"Tell me about the baby," he said.

"What do you want to know?"

"Her name."

"Esme."

"Her surname?"

"Foster, like mine."

His jaw tightened. "And her father?"

Tess stared at him, then looked away, her lips pressed in a thin line. Groups of tourists walked by them on the sidewalk, laughing and chatting in bursts of different languages. She stubbornly refused to look at him, or answer.

"Tess," he demanded, coming close enough to touch her, his tall, broad-shouldered form casting a shadow over her smaller one.

Colorful lights swept over her red hair like a halo as Tess finally looked at him. Her green eyes half filled with hope, half with anger, as she said in a low whisper, "You, Stefano."

Secret Heirs of Billionaires

There are some things money can't buy...

Living life at lightning pace, these magnates are no strangers to stakes at their highest. It seems they've got it all... That is, until they find out that there's an unplanned item to add to their list of accomplishments!

Achieved:

1. Successful business empire.

2. Beautiful women in their bed.

3. *An heir to bear their name?*

Though every billionaire needs to leave his legacy in safe hands, discovering a secret heir shakes up the carefully orchestrated plan in more ways than one!

Uncover their secrets in:

The Greek's Pleasurable Revenge by Andie Brock

The Secret Kept from the Greek by Susan Stephens

Carrying the Spaniard's Child by Jennie Lucas

Kidnapped for the Tycoon's Baby by Louise Fuller

The Greek's Secret Son by Julia James

Claiming His Hidden Heir by Carol Marinelli

The Secret the Italian Claims by Jennie Lucas

Wed for His Secret Heir by Chantelle Shaw

Look out for more stories in the Secret Heirs of Billionaires series coming soon!

Jennie Lucas

—

THE HEIR THE PRINCE SECURES

ISBN-13: 978-1-335-50463-0

The Heir the Prince Secures

First North American Publication 2018

Copyright © 2018 by Jennie Lucas

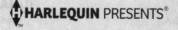

HARLEQUIN PRESENTS®

Recycling programs
for this product may
not exist in your area.

ISBN-13: 978-1-335-50463-0

The Heir the Prince Secures

First North American publication 2018

Copyright © 2018 by Jennie Lucas

Printed in U.S.A.

USA TODAY bestselling author **Jennie Lucas**'s parents owned a bookstore, so she grew up surrounded by books, dreaming about faraway lands. A fourth-generation Westerner, she went east at sixteen to boarding school on a scholarship, wandered the world, got married, then finally worked her way through college before happily returning to her hometown. A 2010 RITA® Award finalist and 2005 Golden Heart® Award winner, she lives in Idaho with her husband and children.

Books by Jennie Lucas

Harlequin Presents

One Night With Consequences

Claiming His Nine-Month Consequence
The Consequence of His Vengeance

Secret Heirs of Billionaires

Carrying the Spaniard's Child
The Secret the Italian Claims

Wedlocked!

Baby of His Revenge

Visit the Author Profile page
at Harlequin.com for more titles.

Dedication

To Katharine, who inspires me every day, and who
daily shows how the impossible can be achieved
with both kindness and grace.

Dear Reader,

How far would you go for love?

Tess Foster, a romantic, kindhearted orphan, has dreamed of falling in love all her life. When a handsome Sicilian stranger seduces her one magical night, she thinks her dream has come true. Instead, she wakes up alone, pregnant and abandoned.

But still, Tess has faith. Until, a year later, she finally learns the heartbreaking reason Prince Stefano never returned—because he didn't love her.

How can she tell him about their baby? Will her heart be permanently broken? Or will her faith in love be rewarded?

This is the second book in a trilogy about three single mothers who are all very different, but have one thing in common: they've never told any of the powerful billionaire fathers about their babies. Hallie's story was *The Secret the Italian Claims*. The trilogy will finish with Lola's story in November, *The Baby the Billionaire Demands*.

I loved writing these stories about three vibrant, different women and the powerful, untamable men who have finally met their match. I hope you love them, too.

With warmest wishes,

Jennie

CHAPTER ONE

LOVE MEANT EVERYTHING to Tess Foster.

Not just love. *Romance*. Pink roses. Castles and hearts.

As a lonely teenager living in the attic of her aunt and uncle's Brooklyn bakery, Tess tried to keep her romantic dreams secret. In a modern world of easy hookups and one-night stands, it was embarrassing, even shameful, to be an idealistic virgin waiting for true love. As other girls giggled over their first fumbling sexual experiences in the back seats of cars, Tess kept quiet and hoped no one would notice that she spent her own Saturday nights with dusty books in the library, dreaming of handsome princes.

She'd known, even then, that when she finally gave herself to a man, it would only be to someone she truly loved. She'd wear white on her wedding day and lose her virginity on their honeymoon. She'd settle for nothing less than the fairy tale.

Then, at twenty-four, she met Stefano.

One moment, she'd been working as a waitress at a glamorous cocktail party hosted by a Spanish media mogul. Carrying a silver tray of champagne flutes through a crowd of movie stars and tycoons, Tess had been lost in thought, worrying whether she'd be able to afford another semester of design school.

Then a handsome stranger's dark, smoldering gaze had pierced her heart, making her lose her breath.

That had been it. That one look from him had almost brought her to her knees.

Because no one had ever looked at her like that. It was as if Tess, the hopeless, invisible wallflower, had suddenly become the most desirable, fascinating woman in all the world.

And the man who was looking at her...

Dark and sexy, he'd stood arrogantly apart, his perfectly cut tuxedo a mere veneer of civilization over his powerful, muscular body. His dark eyes had burned through her as he came toward her, moving with an almost feline grace.

"Buonasera," he'd said huskily.

Tess had turned the silver tray toward him so fast the flutes nearly knocked over. Her voice had squeaked. "Champagne?"

"No." With a sensual smile, he'd glanced at the martini already in his hand. "I don't want champagne."

"Something else, then?"

His voice was husky, with the barest trace of an accent. "I want your name."

And that had been the start of the most spectacular night of Tess's life. When she'd finished her shift at the party, he'd whisked her off in his chauffeured town car to an elegant, romantic dinner at the most exclusive restaurant in New York. Afterward, he'd suggested they go dancing. When she'd said she didn't have a dress, he'd stopped at a designer boutique and bought her one that sparkled and swayed against her skin.

She'd tried to resist, but she couldn't. Not when he'd looked at her like that.

Tess had danced in his arms for hours before he'd kissed her, leaving her intoxicated, breathless. He'd invited her to his suite at the luxurious Leighton Hotel. Looking into his dark, hungry eyes, she'd known only one answer.

"Yes," she'd whispered.

In just one night, he'd ruthlessly taken her virginity. And more than that: he'd dazzled her lonely, romantic heart into loving him.

But the next morning, waking up alone in the cold, gray dawn, she realized that she'd never even learned his full name.

A few weeks later, she'd found out she was pregnant. Her uncle had been furious, her aunt disappointed in her.

For the last fourteen months, even as Tess's two best friends, Hallie Hatfield and Lola Price, had rolled their eyes, she'd stubbornly insisted that Stefano would someday return to claim her and their baby. After all, even if she didn't know his last name, he knew hers. Stefano could find her anytime he wanted.

If he hadn't come yet, there had to be a good reason. Maybe he had amnesia, or his plane had crashed on a desert island. Those things happened, didn't they? Tess imagined every reason she could think of, except for the obvious one. Her friends thought she was nuts.

But Tess had to believe Stefano would return. Because, otherwise, she'd surrendered all her dreams for nothing. She'd given up her chance for a career, for marriage, for one love that would last her whole life—all for a one-night stand that had left her pregnant, abandoned and alone.

If Stefano didn't come back, it would mean the world was a cold and unforgiving place, and all the fairy tales her mother had read her as a child were wrong. Tess didn't want to live in a world like that. So she'd done her best to believe.

Suddenly, tonight, she couldn't.

Not for one more second.

Tess's shoulders drooped as she wearily pushed her five-month-old baby's stroller out of the Campania Hotel New York. It was ten o'clock on a warm, humid night in early September, but the night was just getting started. The streets were crowded with people leaving restaurants and streaming out of Broadway theaters, their faces animated and bright as they passed beneath the sparkling lights of the hotel's porte cochere.

Tess felt empty and sad. She'd just watched her friend Hallie sing at her husband's luxury hotel. After Hallie's amazing performance, Cristiano had publicly declared his love for his wife.

She was glad for Hallie, truly she was. Her friend deserved every happiness, especially after what she'd gone through. Normally, Tess would have told herself that seeing a couple so deeply in love proved that it might still happen for her, too.

But not tonight.

She'd been up since four that morning, working at her uncle's bakery while also caring for her baby. She felt sweaty and exhausted. Tendrils of her long red hair were plastered to her neck. Even Tess's jaunty handmade outfit, a vintage-style shirt and midi pencil skirt with mixing patterns, was wrinkled. She looked down at her adorable sleeping baby, her plump cheeks and dark hair, and a hard lump rose to her throat.

For over a year, she'd ignored her uncle's criticism, her aunt's disappointed sighs and her friends' teasing. She'd told herself Stefano would come back to her. But after seeing Hallie and Cristiano together, so happy together in their own little world, Tess had realized she was fooling herself.

Give it up. A memory came of Lola's tart voice. *He's never coming back, Tess.*

Tess stopped. As streams of people passed by her stroller on both sides of the sidewalk, she savagely wiped tears off her cheeks. She'd planned to take the subway back to Brooklyn with her baby rather than ask Hallie for a ride and risk crying in front of her. Her friends always teased her about being too cheerful and optimistic. She couldn't let them know how she really felt inside.

But that was wrong. Hallie was her friend, and Tess had left without so much as a farewell. Taking a deep breath, she tried to smooth her face into a smile. She'd go back inside now and congratulate Hallie. And if she asked why Tess was crying—

As Tess started to turn, she walked into a wall.

Not a wall. *A man.*

For a second, she saw stars from the blunt force of hitting her head against his chest. Dizzy, she shook her head, mortified.

"I'm so sorry," she blurted out. "It was my fault—"

Then she saw him.

For a second, Tess couldn't breathe. Her heart pounded in her throat as she tilted her head back to stare at the man's handsome face, his sharp cheekbones and jawline shadowed by the lights of the hotel's grand porte cochere.

Tall and dark-haired, the man wore a sleek black

jacket that emphasized his broad shoulders, and trousers that fit snugly over powerful thighs. His tailored shirt was open a single button at the neck.

He wasn't strictly handsome, perhaps. His aquiline profile was a bit too arrogant, the set of his square jaw too thuggish. But he gave the impression of intense masculine beauty. His face was arresting, his body powerful, giving him the look of a dark angel.

The man's eyes widened, the irises so dark as to be almost black against his olive-colored skin.

Tess's lips parted.

"Stefano?" she whispered, gripping the handle of the stroller for balance. "Is it really you?"

She knew those dark eyes. That handsome face. Those cruel, sensual lips. She knew every bit of him. She'd dreamed of him, day and night, for over a year.

"Tess," he murmured.

His low, husky voice caressed the short syllable of her name. So he was real, then. *He was real.*

"You came back for me," she whispered. Joy rose inside her, brighter than all the lights of Broadway and Times Square put together. "You came back!"

His jaw tightened. He looked down at her from his lofty height, his broad shoulders towering over her. "What do you want?"

What did she want? She wanted to throw her

arms around him, to cry out her happiness to all the world. After a difficult year, with everyone mocking her, this proved that happy endings still happened as long as your heart was true and you had faith. She'd been right!

But, as Tess moved to throw her arms around him, Stefano stepped back from her.

Something was wrong. She bit her lip, bewildered. "I am so happy to see you. Did you just get back?"

"Get back?"

"To New York." When he didn't answer, she continued with a blush, "Our night together, you said that you had to return to Europe but you'd be back soon—"

"Oh. Yes." His chiseled face was dark with shadow beneath his hard cheekbones as the lights of passing traffic moved past them on the avenue. "I've been in New York often this summer. And now for Fashion Week, of course."

"You've been here all this time?" A chill went through her as her joy withered inside her. She whispered, "And you didn't want to see me?"

Stefano frowned. His voice was a low baritone. "I liked you very much, Tess. It was an amazing night. But…"

"But?" she croaked.

Coming closer, he looked down at her, his dark eyes glittering. "But it was just a night."

To him it had just been a one-night stand, nothing more? One night, easily enjoyed and easily forgotten?

Tess's cheeks went hot as she remembered telling him in bed, in the hushed quiet before dawn with their naked bodies still intertwined, "I'm already falling in love with you."

In her innocence, Tess had meant every word. She'd been intoxicated by sensual pleasure she'd never imagined. In just twelve hours, he'd given her the most intense happiness of her life, more emotion and joy and beauty than she'd known for twelve *years* before. If that wasn't love, what was?

Now, looking at his coldly handsome face, Tess realized that her honesty had been a fatal mistake. Because when she woke the next morning, he'd been gone.

"Your Highness!" A young girl caught up behind him on the sidewalk. She was obviously a model—tall, slender, dark-haired and incredibly beautiful in a white dress that set off her dark skin. She held out a small notebook to Stefano. "You forgot this."

"Thanks, Kebe," he said gruffly.

She tossed her dark curls. "See you in Paris."

She left in a perfect catwalk stride.

"Who was that?" Tess whispered.

"A friend," he said. His dark eyes flicked briefly to the sleeping baby in the stroller behind her.

"Well. It was nice to see you again." His expression was cool. Courteous. Distant. "Goodbye."

Pain and shock spread through Tess's body, making her knees shake.

He hadn't been looking for her.

At all.

He'd rejected her long ago. She just hadn't known it till now. Stinging tears filled her eyes.

All this time she'd dreamed of him as a romantic hero who was desperate to return to her. The truth was that Stefano simply hadn't wanted to see her again.

Over the last year, as Tess had dropped out of college to work full-time at her uncle's bakery, struggling to provide and care for their baby, Stefano had been traveling the world, enjoying himself. In fact, it seemed he'd just been out on a date with a beautiful girl who looked barely eighteen. Whom he'd promised to see again in Paris.

Stricken, she looked at him with tears in her eyes.

Stefano's expression hardened. "Tess, it was for the best."

Wordlessly shaking her head, she backed away. For so long, she'd held out hope, imagining one perfect love brought by destiny, by fate. She'd remained faithful to Stefano's memory, dreaming of the day her handsome prince would return on a white horse to whisk her and the baby to his castle.

But Stefano was no prince.

Her friends and family had been right.

Tess gripped the stroller for support as anguish and exhaustion punched through her.

They'd been right.

"Come now. Don't act like your heart's broken," he said sharply. "How long did it take you to get over me? A few days?"

"How can you say that?" she whispered.

He looked pointedly at the baby in the stroller. "She's yours, isn't she?"

Yes. And yours. The words rose inside her, but got caught in her throat.

"And what about her father?" he demanded. "How would he feel if he knew you were here now, talking to me?"

"You tell me."

"How would I know?" Reaching out, he cupped her cheek. For a moment, in spite of everything, she closed her eyes, shivering at his touch as a flash of heat pulsed through her.

Stefano dropped his hand. "Let's not try to make more of our night than it was." He glanced at the baby. "Obviously, you quickly moved on. So did I. Our night was enjoyable enough. But it was meaningless."

Enjoyable enough?

Meaningless?

It was the final straw. She felt a flash of despair, the destructive kind that froze to the bone.

"Our night didn't mean anything to you?" Heart in her throat, she whispered, "You changed my life."

"Sorry," he said coldly.

She felt the word like a bullet.

"Fine." She closed her eyes briefly, shuddering. "We'll survive alone."

Knees shaking, she turned and walked away from him as fast as she could, away from her broken heart, from her shame that she'd so foolishly believed in the fairy tale. She fled the glittering lights of the Campania toward a shadowy side street, desperate to reach the far-off subway entrance, where she could sob in peace.

Prince Stefano Zacco di Gioreale stared after Tess, shocked by the jolt of her words, by the raw emotion he'd seen on her face and, most of all, by his body's reaction to seeing her again.

Tess Foster was even more beautiful than he remembered. He'd lied when he'd said he'd quickly moved on. The truth was that he'd spent the last year trying not to recall her hauntingly lovely heart-shaped face, her red hair, her bright emerald eyes, her sweet pink lips. He'd tried to forget her lush body and the way she'd felt naked in his arms.

Most of all, he'd tried to erase the memory of

her intense, heartfelt whisper the next morning. *I'm already falling in love with you.*

For the last year, he'd done his best to forget. He'd told himself he had. Still, when he'd returned to New York in July to preside over the launch of Mercurio's flagship store, there was a reason he'd chosen to stay at the Campania Hotel rather than return to the Leighton, which had all those sweet, savage memories of their night together.

From the moment he'd first seen her carrying a tray of champagne at Rodrigo Cabrera's cocktail party, he'd known he wanted her. He'd felt drawn to Tess in a way he'd never experienced before. Or since.

He'd made it his mission to seduce her. As beautiful and vivacious as Tess was, it had never occurred to him she might be a virgin. Not until it was too late, not until he'd already pushed himself into her, both of them gasping with ecstasy. His body shivered at the memory.

He'd felt guilty afterward, though. There was a reason he didn't seduce virgins. They fell in love too easily and cloyingly imagined a future that bored Stefano to tears. He avoided them at all costs. Virgins didn't know how to play the game. Play it? They often didn't even know there *was* a game.

His worst fears had been proven true when, after the most spectacular sexual experience of his life,

Tess had ruined everything with her outrageous declaration of love.

So he'd left. He took no pleasure in it. He would have preferred to see her again for many more sensual nights.

But she'd given him no choice. If she was already imagining herself in love with him after *twelve hours*, what would she do when he eventually ended their affair? Throw herself off the Empire State Building?

So Stefano had left. For her own good. He had nothing to offer a dreamy-eyed idealist with a heart full of love. Better to set her free immediately, before anyone got hurt.

The existence of the baby proved he'd made the right choice. Judging by the infant's size, Tess couldn't have waited long before she took another lover.

An image came to Stefano of another man taking Tess in his arms, doing exactly what he'd done, possessing her in furious, desperate need, in a hot tangle of limbs and sweat and pleasure. Scowling, he pushed the thought away.

At least Stefano had used protection. Obviously, the other man hadn't been so careful. The unknown man had gotten her pregnant with his dark-eyed baby.

He was surprised Tess wasn't wearing a wedding ring. He would have thought a romantic girl like her wouldn't be satisfied with anything less than happily-ever-after.

Stefano, a billionaire prince who'd been raised in a Sicilian castle, didn't believe in such fairy tales.

But he couldn't stop his eyes from watching Tess hungrily as her small figure disappeared down the dark street, her shoulders drooping and red hair flying as she pushed the stroller ahead of her.

Stefano's hand tingled. Raising his hand, he looked at his fingertips beneath the hotel's bright lights.

All he'd done was touch her cheek. That brief, simple touch had scorched his hand. All the emotion and desire he'd repressed for a year had suddenly roared into greedy life, burning him like a fire. Shocked, he'd dropped his hand.

As he watched Tess disappear down the block, he felt a new sense of loss. Why? Why did he still feel so drawn to her? He'd had beautiful women in his bed before. Why couldn't he forget this particular one?

Stefano forced himself to turn away. It was better this way, he repeated to himself. He started to walk toward the hotel's entrance. He stopped.

Something didn't make sense. He frowned.

If Tess was so happy in her new relationship, raising another man's child, why had she been so overjoyed to see Stefano? She'd looked at him like unicorns were dancing on rainbows. Like all her dreams had suddenly come true.

Our night didn't mean anything to you?

He could still hear the tremble of her voice, still see the shadows cross her lovely, troubled face.

You changed my life.

And as she'd spoken she'd looked away.

Toward the stroller.

Toward her baby.

Her dark-haired, plump-cheeked baby.

"We'll survive alone," she'd said.

We. Not *I.*

A low growl came from the back of Stefano's throat. Turning, he pursued her grimly down the street.

Even with his longer stride, it took him time to catch up with her. He reached her at the end of the dark street, almost at the edge of Times Square. Grabbing Tess by the shoulder, he forced her to face him as the colorful lights of the electronic billboards lit up the sky brilliantly behind her.

"Wait," he ground out.

Tess had been crying, he saw. Her green eyes glittered like emeralds in her pale face. She lifted her chin fiercely. "Wait for what? For you?" She wiped her eyes. "What do you think I've been doing for the last year?"

Her voice was quietly accusing. Against his

will, Stefano's gaze fell to her full, pink lips, and lower still.

Tess's hourglass figure should have been illegal in the modern world. Her flowy long-sleeved blouse was tucked into a midi pencil skirt, like a sexpot librarian. It showed her curves to perfection—her full breasts, tiny waist, and big hips a man could wrap his hands around. Her red hair tumbled over her shoulders, the color of roses, the color of fire.

She was different from any other woman he'd ever seen. He wanted her. Even more than before. More than he'd ever wanted any woman.

With all his relationships over the years, his mistresses always knew love wasn't part of the equation. He only dated experienced, beautiful women he enjoyed having in his bed and on his arm. In return, they enjoyed his body, his prestige and the lifestyle he could provide.

If he was honest with himself, it had all grown rather tedious. Mechanical. He'd started to wonder which of them was using the other one more. Which was why he'd stopped having love affairs, even one-night stands, after his night with Tess. He hadn't wanted any other woman.

Why? Why did he want only her? Was it simply because he knew she was forbidden? Surely he couldn't be selfish enough to desire something only because he knew he couldn't have it?

Even now, he found his gaze lingering on her full hips, her plump, generous breasts. Her colorful outfit, with its ridiculously whimsical fabric, set off her amazing figure. His eyes lifted from her breasts to her bare collarbone, up her swanlike throat to her lovely heart-shaped face.

Her pink tongue nervously licked the corners of her mouth. His whole body felt electrified. All he wanted to do was kiss her.

Clenching his hands at his sides, he forced himself to turn toward the dark-haired baby in the stroller. She was still sleeping peacefully, her old-fashioned, collared dress half-covered with a blanket, clutching a stuffed giraffe toy in her plump arms.

No. She couldn't be. But even as Stefano told himself there was no resemblance, suspicion pulsed through his body, tightening his chest from his shoulders to his taut belly.

"Tell me about the baby," he said.

"What do you want to know?"

"Her name."

"Esme."

"Her surname?"

"Foster, like mine."

His jaw tightened. "And her father?"

Tess stared at him, then looked away, her lips pressed in a thin line. Groups of tourists walked by them on the sidewalk, laughing and chatting in bursts of different languages. She stubbornly refused to look at him, or answer.

"Tess," he demanded, coming close enough to touch her, his tall, broad-shouldered form casting a shadow over her smaller one.

Colorful lights swept over her red hair like a halo, as Tess finally looked at him. Her green eyes were half filled with hope, half with anger, as she said in a low whisper, "You, Stefano."

CHAPTER TWO

TESS HAD IMAGINED so many times the moment she'd finally tell Stefano about their precious baby.

She'd pictured him crying out with joy and kissing her passionately, then taking Esme proudly in his arms. She'd dreamed of him falling to his knees to plead for her forgiveness for neglecting her so long—unavoidable as he was trapped on the desert island—and then begging her to be his bride.

She'd never imagined this.

"No." Stefano's black eyes were wide as he took a single step back on the sidewalk, his sleek jacket and trousers blending into the dark shadows. He looked down at the sleeping baby. "It can't be true."

Her heart twisted. She whispered, "It's true."

"How can you be sure?"

She hid the pang she felt at his careless insult. "You're the only man I've ever been with, Stefano. Ever, in my whole life."

"But we were careful. We used protection."

Stefano's hard, handsome face looked so shocked Tess almost felt bad for him. She almost wanted

to comfort him, to tell him everything would be all right.

But even Tess's tender heart couldn't quite manage that. Not when the man she'd waited for all this time, the man in whom she'd placed her hope and faith, was making his rejection so clear—not just of Tess, but of Esme, too. She lifted her chin.

"I was surprised, too," she said evenly. "But it turns out condoms aren't always one hundred percent effective."

"Why didn't you tell me?" he demanded.

Her jaw dropped.

"How could I? I didn't know your last name or where you lived." She lifted her chin. "You always knew where to find me. You just didn't want to. I waited for over a year, believing you'd return." She hated the tears rising behind her eyes. "Everyone mocked me and teased me for it. I was in love with you, having your baby, and I didn't even know your last name!"

Tess was relieved for the distraction when her baby started to whimper. Blinking rapidly, she picked up the stuffed giraffe Esme had dropped on the sidewalk, then placed it tenderly in the baby's arms.

"It's Zacco," Stefano said abruptly. "My last name."

She looked up. "Zacco? Like the fashion brand?"

Even Tess had heard of the legendary luxury

brand, famous for its haute couture and iconic handbags printed with flamboyant interlocking Zs.

"Yes," he said, then shook his head. "My great-great-grandfather started it. I will buy it back soon."

"You don't own it anymore? How could you lose rights to a company named after your own family?"

His jaw tightened, and he looked at their baby. "How could you get pregnant?"

The coldness in his voice pierced her heart. It was one thing for Stefano to treat Tess badly; another to be scornful of their baby.

Sweet five-month-old Esme, so plump and adorable and always happy, at least when she wasn't tired or hungry or teething, was already the person Tess loved most on this planet. Esme was her whole reason for living.

"I've just told you that you have a daughter." Tess felt a wave of dizziness that nearly brought her to her knees. She reached wildly for the stroller handle, gripping it tight so she didn't fall. "And that's all you have to say?"

His eyes narrowed. "How do I know she's mine?"

"Stop asking that! I told you!"

"I need more proof than just your word."

A white-haired couple holding theater playbills

walked past, hand in hand. Seeing the way the couple smiled at each other, Tess's heart ached. That was what she'd wanted for herself. A lifetime love.

She'd wanted it so badly she'd been desperate to believe Stefano was the one, in spite of all evidence to the contrary. She'd be regretting it the rest of her life.

"Forget it." Her throat ached as she turned away. "We don't need you."

Stefano ground out, "I'm sorry if I hurt you—"

"Sorry?" Her voice trembled. "You're not sorry!"

"You're wrong," he said harshly. "I'm sorry I didn't realize you were a virgin until too late. Sorry you imagined yourself in love with me when you didn't even know me. Sorry you're now trying to claim your baby is mine!"

"Claim?" Tess's tears blurred his image as colorful flashing lights from the billboards of Times Square moved over his hard, handsome face. "You're right," she whispered. "I don't know you."

She couldn't believe she'd been so horribly wrong about everything. Even now, Stefano still looked like a handsome dream—tall and powerful in his sleek suit. Even his scent, like Italian oranges and hot summer nights, made her heart twist with longing and grief for what she could not have, what had never truly existed.

Reaching out, he gripped her shoulders. His dark eyes burned through her. "I never promised a future."

As she felt the weight of his hands on her shoulders, electricity pulsed through her, leaving her breathless.

Her gaze fell to his cruel, sensual lips as she whispered, "I know."

She heard his intake of breath. His grip on her shoulders tightened. "Stop it."

"What?"

"You know what."

His eyes were dark pools of hunger. As their eyes locked, sensual awareness coursed through her, sending sparks up and down her body, causing tension to coil low and deep inside her. Unthinkingly, she licked the corners of her lips. First one side, then the other.

With a low growl, he pulled her hard against his body and savagely lowered his mouth to hers.

She was lost in a rush of ecstasy as desire and anguished longing roared through her blood. She surrendered to the pleasure, to his power, his strength, relishing the feel of his arms wrapped around her.

Then, as if from a distance, she heard a choked moan rising from her own throat, wistful and broken, and she remembered how he'd just crushed her heart to a million pieces.

No. No!

Ripping away, she stared up at him in horror, her lips still tingling with pleasure, her heart bruised by that brief fiery joy.

"Don't you dare kiss me!"

His expression changed. "Tess—"

"Leave me alone." Her voice wobbled. She was afraid she might burst into sobs, and baby Esme's tired, hungry whine was threatening to become a wail.

Tess wiped her mouth with her sleeve, trying to forget the sweet taste of his lips, but she couldn't. A tsunami of grief and regret and exhaustion roared through her, leaving her trembling and dizzy.

She suddenly knew she wasn't going to make it to the subway. She was going to collapse right here on the street in front of the man who'd caused it all.

No. She had to somehow get back to her friends. She didn't care anymore if Hallie and Lola said *I told you so*. They were her only hope now that her whole world was falling down around her.

Swaying unsteadily, she turned, stumbling as she pushed the stroller back down the way she'd come. She could see the distant lights of the Campania at the end of the street.

"Tess." Catching up with her, Stefano grabbed the handle of the stroller. "Stop. Damn you."

His face was in shadow. The lights of a single passing car seemed long, smudging before her eyes. The world swam around her as the last of her strength fled. She closed her eyes.

For the last year, she'd tried to have faith while she waited for Stefano to come back and save her. But now that he'd returned, all he'd done was take away the dreams that had sustained her.

"Please," she whispered, blinking fast, feeling dizzy and sick. "Don't."

He frowned, looking down at her. "What's wrong?"

The dizziness increased, building to a pounding roar in her ears. She felt her knees start to collapse.

His strong arms shot out, keeping her from plummeting to the sidewalk. "Tess?"

The last thing she saw was the worried gleam of his dark eyes as the night folded in around her.

Tess was swaying, cradled in someone's arms.

Her eyelids fluttered open, then went wide with shock. Stefano was carrying her in his arms, against his hard chest. They'd already reached the end of the block and were almost at the hotel.

"Esme," Tess gasped, twisting in his arms.

"She's safe, behind us." Stefano's voice was surprisingly gentle. Peeking over his broad shoulders, she saw a doorman she recognized from the Campania pushing the stroller. She'd met Dalton several times when she'd visited Hallie at the hotel. He gave her an encouraging smile.

"It's all right, Miss Foster." He glanced down at the baby. "She's right here."

"Thank you, Dalton," she whispered. Then she glared at the powerful man carrying her. "Put me down."

"No." Stefano kept walking. His handsome face was implacable. "You fainted on the street."

"I'm better now," she said, struggling in his arms. "Put me down."

His arms tightened around her. "When is the last time you ate?"

Tess struggled to remember. "This morning?"

"Aren't you sure?"

She shook her head weakly. "I started work at four. The bakery opens at six, and my uncle doesn't approve of eating in front of customers. On breaks I'm busy with Esme." She looked away. "I meant to eat something tonight, but I had to feed Esme. So I just had a glass of champagne." She put her hand on her forehead, still feeling dizzy. "She's been teething, so I didn't sleep much last night…"

Stefano shook his head as they approached the hotel's gilded revolving door. "I'm taking you upstairs until a doctor looks you over."

"It's not necessary," she said desperately. The last thing she wanted was to be vulnerable—in his arms or his hotel suite.

"A doctor," he repeated, his glare fierce. "He'll

make sure you're all right. Then we'll get a paternity test."

She stiffened in his arms even as he carried her through the door. How could he ask for a test? Her word should be enough!

The grand lobby of the Campania was huge and luxurious, with midcentury decor and turn-of-the-century architecture. Molded plaster ceilings with crystal chandeliers soared high above the marble floor and paneled walls. Glamorous hotel guests and patrons crowded around the gleaming oak bar at the center.

Tess felt conspicuous as they walked past. They made a strange parade, with Stefano carrying her in his arms and the doorman pushing the stroller behind them. People turned to stare.

A group of gorgeous, very tall, very thin young women gaped at them openly from their table at the lobby bar. *Models*, Tess thought. They were their own tribe in this city, and you could always tell.

"Good evening, Your Highness," a man said as he passed, his eyes wide.

"Your Highness," a woman greeted him, looking as if she were dying to ask all kinds of questions.

Stefano responded only with a nod and kept walking.

"Your Highness?" Tess looked up at him. "That

other girl called you that earlier. I thought it was a joke."

"I'm technically a prince," he said tersely.

"Technically?"

"Italy is a republic. Aristocratic titles are now merely honorary," he said flatly. "But my ancestors have been princes of Gioreale for hundreds of years."

"Gioreale is a place?"

"In Sicily. Once it was an important market village. Now it's a ghost of its former self. That is what I am." His lips curved. "Prince of ghosts."

Prince of ghosts. She thought she saw something haunted in his eyes. What was it? Emptiness? Pain? Despair?

"Miss Foster." Mr. Loggia, the hotel's general manager, came forward with an anxious frown. "What has happened? Are you injured?"

"She fainted, sir," the doorman said from behind them. "Prince Stefano alerted me from down the street, and I rushed to help."

"I see." The manager, who'd never been anything but kind to Tess, turned to Stefano with a scowl. "What did you do?"

Stefano replied coldly in Italian, and the manager responded in the same language, lifting his chin.

Mr. Loggia whirled to face her. "Is he taking you against your will?"

Stefano bit out something in Italian that sounded very rude.

"Miss Foster?" the manager demanded.

Tess felt Stefano's strong arms tighten around her, pressing her body against his powerful chest. As she looked at him, her lips tingled from his savage kiss by Times Square.

"No," she admitted, her heart in her throat. "He's right. I fainted."

Stefano turned icily to the manager. "I'm taking her to my suite, Loggia. Send up the doctor. And room service. What would you like?" he asked Tess.

Food. He was talking about food? She shook her head dimly. "I don't care."

"Are you sure you don't want me to call Mrs. Moretti?" the manager asked her with a frown.

For a moment, Tess was tempted to take the offered escape. Then she glanced back at her whining, hungry baby in the stroller. She knew what it was like to grow up without a father. If there was even a chance that Stefano wanted to be part of their baby's life, didn't she have to find out?

Even if that meant she had to take a paternity test to make him finally believe her.

"It's all right, Mr. Loggia," she said, quietly resigned. "I want to go with him."

She felt Stefano's arms relax slightly.

"If you're sure," the manager said, looking between them in disbelief. "I'll have room service send up your usual at once. And the hotel doctor, as well."

"Grazie," Stefano bit out sardonically, and turned away, carrying her to the elevator. The doorman pushed the stroller behind them.

"Mr. Loggia doesn't seem to like you much," Tess said.

"No," he agreed, not seeming perturbed about it. "In spite of the fact I'm their highest-paying guest. But his bastard boss despises me."

"Cristiano hates you?" Tess blinked in surprise. "Why would he?"

"You know Moretti?"

"His wife Hallie is one of my best friends."

"Ah." He shrugged. "He and I were drivers in a charity car race last year. We were fighting for the win. His car was in my way, so I—very gently—bumped him over."

"You hit his car?"

"He was blocking me. Cheating. He left me no choice. After I won, he tried to punch me in the face."

Tess couldn't imagine Cristiano losing his temper. He seemed so nice, especially tonight, when he'd declared his love for Hallie. "He *punched* you?"

"I said he tried to." Stefano hid a smug smile.

"His friends held him back. I felt no need to return his attack. He simply couldn't accept that his attempts to sabotage me in the race had failed and I'd still managed to win."

"Winning isn't everything."

He looked at her in disbelief. "Of course it is."

The elevator door opened, and he carried her inside, with the doorman and the stroller behind them.

"If you dislike Cristiano Moretti so much, why do you stay at his hotel?"

"Because it amuses me to force him and his manager to serve me."

"They might spit in your food."

"They would not dare. Would they, Dalton?"

"Certainly not," the doorman replied indignantly. He added with a grin, "You tip far too well for that, Your Highness."

Stefano returned his grin, then looked at Tess. "Besides. I know Moretti, and he has too much pride in his hotel to ever serve any guest badly. Even me. He contents himself by merely marking up my bill to an exorbitant amount."

Tess glanced at Dalton, feeling awkward to be discussing Cristiano like this, in front of one of his employees. She asked Stefano helplessly, "Don't you mind all the conflict?"

"No."

"You like it!" she accused.

Stefano said with a careless smile, "A man can be measured by the quality of his enemies."

"My mother used to say that you can be measured by the strength of your love for family and friends."

He snorted. "That is the most sentimental thing I have ever heard in my life. What was your mother's profession?"

"Theater actress." A flash of grief went through her as she thought of her loving but impractical mother, dragging her as a child through summer stock plays and minor roles in small New England towns. She added softly, "Though she was never very successful at it."

"And your father?"

She felt a different kind of grief. "My mother raised me alone." She raised her chin. "You can set me down anytime. I'm perfectly able to stand."

"Not yet," he said shortly. "Not until we reach my suite."

With a sigh, Tess watched the elevator numbers go higher. Her baby gave another soft whine from the stroller. Esme was tired and she needed to be fed. At this rate, they wouldn't be home till midnight. Tess hated the thought of coming home so late and facing her uncle's wrath.

The elevator door slid open, and Stefano carried her down the hall. As Dalton held open the door, he took her into the suite.

Tess looked around her in amazement.

The royal suite was lavish, spread out across the corner of one of the Campania's highest floors. Floor-to-ceiling windows provided views of Manhattan from every room. Carrying her into the elegant living room, which had a grand piano in the corner, Stefano finally set her down gently on a white sofa.

"Are you cold? Do you want a blanket?"

"You're being ridiculous. I'm not an invalid." She started to get up from the sofa, then felt dizzy and fell back against the pillows. "I just want my baby—"

Without a word, Stefano went back to the foyer. She saw him reach into his pocket.

"Thank you," he said, handing Dalton a folded fistful of bills.

"You're so welcome," the doorman replied fervently, and, with a respectful nod toward Tess, he left.

Kneeling in front of the stroller, Stefano unbuckled the unhappy baby, lifting her up into his arms.

Father and daughter looked at each other with the same dark eyes. Esme's whimpering stopped. The baby reached out a flailing arm and touched her father's face.

Stefano laughed, looking down at her. His expression changed. It became almost…tender.

Watching them, Tess felt her heart twist in her chest.

Clearing his throat, he returned to the sofa and placed the baby in Tess's arms. Esme immediately nuzzled toward her.

"Do you want anything else?" he asked.

With a lump in her throat, Tess shook her head. She couldn't tell him the truth.

There was something she wanted, almost more than she could bear. Watching Stefano hold her baby, she'd wanted him to be the man she'd once believed him to be.

Two hours later, as Stefano shut the door behind the departing doctor, he looked back across the shadows of the royal suite. Tess and the baby had fallen asleep on the white sofa with the wide view of sparkling city lights. Beside her, there was an empty tray, with only crumbs left of her sandwich and soup. She'd gulped down three glasses of water, too.

Slowly he came closer, looking down at her. Even now, as Tess slept, he could see the dark smudges beneath her eyes. Her beautiful face looked exhausted. She'd fallen asleep in the few minutes he'd spoken privately with the doctor.

"She needs rest," the doctor had told him at the door. "She's been working too hard. She has nothing left in reserve. Take care of her."

Tess had such power over him. Stefano could still feel their kiss and remember how it had felt to hold her soft body in his arms, to plunder the sweet softness of her lips. He wanted her. And she was here. In his suite.

His gaze shifted to the bedroom door at the end of the hall.

Shaking his head hard, he pushed the thought away. Only one thing mattered now. It had nothing to do with sex and everything to do with honor.

Stefano's gaze slid to the baby still cuddled in Tess's arms. Esme had fallen asleep hours ago, as soon as she'd been changed and fed. That seemed appropriate given that it was past midnight. He didn't know much about children, but even in his own disastrous childhood, Stefano had always been tucked safely in his bed every night by a nanny. For all his parents' selfishness, they'd managed at least that much for their only child.

Which was more than Stefano himself could say if the paternity test proved Esme was his daughter. Had he unknowingly abandoned Tess, pregnant with his baby, without any money or any means to contact him?

His hands tightened.

He'd never wanted to hurt her. He'd tried his best to protect her, by leaving her. Before her love for him could get any worse.

Stefano still wasn't sure what love was, exactly.

Was love real, and was he deficient in some way since he'd never felt it? Or was it an illusion, and were other people deluding themselves?

He preferred to think the latter.

But he'd never known a woman like Tess. The women he dated were usually exactly like him—selfish and ruthless, looking out only for themselves and determined to win at any cost.

Was Tess truly so innocent that she'd given him her heart and virginity, then raised his baby with faith he would return, loving him with such unimaginable loyalty?

He'd never known anyone that unselfish. Ever. Including—and especially—his own parents.

Stefano's father, Prince Umberto, had only cared about sordid extravagances, and thrilling affairs with women he swore he loved, then quickly discarded. He hadn't just cheated on his wife, he'd cheated on his mistresses. He'd ruined the family's famous company, the luxury Zacco brand, through his neglect, then sold it outright during the divorce.

After that, Stefano's mother, Antonella, had gone on to marry five more times, to progressively younger men, each living off her money during marriage and demanding a fat payout at the end of it. Stefano's parents had been too self-involved to bother personally with the care of their son, choosing to leave him at their castle in Sicily to be raised by paid servants. At twelve, they'd sent him off to an American boarding school, and left him there, even during the summers.

The Zacco legacy, the legendary hundred-year-old company—even the corporate rights to their very *name*—had been lost to his parents' selfishness. After his father's death when Stefano was finishing college at twenty-two, he'd inherited almost nothing: a falling-down castle in Sicily, some heavily mortgaged real estate, and the nearly bankrupt leather goods company that eventually became Mercurio.

In life, it was every man—and every woman—for themselves. Stefano had learned the lesson well. And life was a game he intended to win.

Over the last sixteen years, Stefano had laboriously rebuilt everything his parents had lost. His international conglomerate, Gioreale S.p.A., was now worth billions, containing luxury brands that sold everything from sports cars to champagne to jewels. And he was building the exclusive fashion line, Mercurio.

It was true, Mercurio's launch last year hadn't gone as well as he'd hoped, but he'd just hired a hot new designer, the eccentric, trendy Caspar von Schreck. His first clothing collection would be shown next month at Paris Fashion Week.

And soon, if everything went as planned, Stefano would finally acquire what he wanted most—

he'd buy back the Zacco brand. Everything was coming together.

He should have been happy, or at least pleased.

But the truth was, at thirty-eight, Stefano was feeling strangely tired of all of it. It was why he'd left tonight's party early, even arranging for his driver to give teenage model Kebe Kedane a ride back to her anxiously waiting mother on the Upper West Side.

Once, Stefano had loved the thrill of New York Fashion Week, the parties, the clubs, the gorgeous women. Lately, everything he'd given his life to conquer…left him numb. He found himself wanting something else. Something more.

Taking back the Zacco brand would change everything, he told himself firmly. Next week he'd start negotiations with Fenella Montfort to buy back his family's legacy. Once it was his, he'd finally feel satisfied. He'd finally feel at peace.

He'd finally have won.

"Oh," Tess murmured, yawning as she stirred on the sofa. She blinked, cradling her baby gently as she sat up, rubbing her eyes. "I must have fallen asleep."

"You're tired." He looked down at her. "I'd like you to stay here tonight."

Her cheeks went pink. She looked down shyly, her dark eyelashes fluttering against her skin. "That's very kind of you, but—"

"It's not kind. I want this settled, one way or the other, before I leave for London tomorrow."

"London?"

"For Fashion Week."

She blinked in surprise. "Are you attending all of them?"

"Yes, back to back. New York, London, Milan, Paris." He gave her a humorless smile. "I do own a fashion brand."

"But it's not Zacco?" She said, looking bewildered.

"Mercurio." His smile dropped. "My father sold Zacco almost twenty years ago. I intend to buy it back. I'll start the negotiations in London."

"Good for you." The deal that meant so much to him obviously meant nothing to her. She stretched her shoulders back, drawing her shoulder blades together, which pushed her breasts forward, stretching the fabric of her modest vintage shirt. Unwillingly, his eyes traced over the shape of her breasts. Catching himself, he forced his attention back to her face.

But her eyes were even more dangerous than her body. They were deep emerald pools, like oceans for an unwary man to drown in.

"When will you be back from Europe?"

"I don't know."

Careful not to jostle the sleeping baby in her arms, she rose from the sofa. "Thank you for dinner, and for offering to let me stay, but Esme and I really should be getting home."

She started toward the foyer where the stroller waited, but he moved to block her. "You're not going anywhere."

His voice was harsher than he'd intended. Tess's lips parted, angry sparks rising in her green eyes.

"Please," he said, amending his tone. "I want you to stay. Dr. Miller promised the paternity results first thing in the morning."

"Why should I stay? It'll only prove what I already know. You're Esme's father. I have no reason to wait all night to get the news." She looked at the floor. "I've waited for you long enough."

An unsettled feeling filled Stefano. If she was telling the truth, then it meant he'd unthinkingly, cruelly abandoned her, pregnant with his baby. He couldn't let himself even reflect about what that might mean or the choice he'd have to make.

Stefano came closer. "Please stay. Until we know for sure."

Tess lifted her chin. "I have to get up early tomorrow."

"Again?"

"I work fifty hours a week."

"Why? Does it pay well?"

Tess gave a smile tinged with bitterness. "Minimum wage. Plus room and board for myself and Esme."

"Minimum wage?" He was outraged. "Why would you work so hard for so little?"

"There aren't many jobs I'm qualified for and where I can keep Esme with me."

"You should have stayed in design school."

"Wow," she said sarcastically. "Thank you for pointing that out to me." Her cheeks burned. "But I couldn't afford both tuition and day care, or manage sixteen-hour days of work and school away from her."

Stefano stared at Tess.

He could instantly picture what her life had been like since he'd left her last year, pregnant, penniless and alone. She'd worked a menial job for little pay, giving up her dreams of college, struggling to provide for her baby with no hope for the future.

All because he'd made sure she had no way to contact him ever again.

His stomach clenched. "If what you say is true and she's my child…it will change everything. Surely you know that."

Biting her lip, she glanced down at the sleeping baby in her arms, then said in a small voice, "It would?"

Placing his hands gently on her shoulders, Stefano said quietly, "Please stay, Tess. You're tired and so is Esme. Just stay. You can have the bedroom. I'll sleep on the sofa."

She gave him a startled glance, then looked at

her sleeping baby cuddled against her chest. With visible reluctance, she sighed. "All right. Fine." Going to the stroller, she returned with a diaper bag slung over her shoulder. "Where is the bedroom?"

He felt an unexpected rush of triumph that he'd convinced her to stay. "This way."

Stefano led her down a short hallway to the hotel suite's bedroom with its huge four-poster bed, marble bathroom and view of the sparkling city lights. He pointed toward the bathroom. "There's a new toothbrush, toiletries, everything you might need." He paused uncertainly. "Do you want me to have the concierge send up pajamas? A crib for the baby?"

She shook her head, her eyes looking tired. "Just leave us."

With a nod, Stefano departed, softly closing the door behind him. As he returned to the main room, his shoulders were tense. He felt strangely restless. He played a few notes on the grand piano, then stopped, remembering Tess and the baby were trying to sleep. Turning to the wet bar, he poured himself a short Scotch and went to the windows, looking at the darkly glittering New York night.

Taking a drink, he stared out bleakly into the night, letting the potent forty-year-old Scotch burn down his throat.

Tess. The bright-eyed redhead was different

than any woman he'd ever met, funny and sweet and sexy as hell. The morning he'd woken up in her arms, he'd already been planning to have her in his bed every night until he was satiated with her. Then she'd told him she was falling in love with him, and the whole world had stopped.

Stefano abruptly turned from the window. Work. Work was what he should be focusing on right now. As always.

Setting down his half-empty glass, he grabbed his laptop and sat down on the sofa. Blankly, he read through emails, including reviews of rival companies' shows during New York Fashion Week and details about Mercurio's upcoming event in Paris.

As Stefano read through the reports that had seemed so urgent only hours before, all the analysis and numbers seemed like meaningless symbols on the screen. From the bedroom, he thought he heard Tess's voice singing lullabies to the baby.

His baby.

He didn't know that yet for sure, Stefano reminded himself fiercely. Yet—he thought of baby Esme's dark eyes—he *knew.*

And if it was proved that five-month-old Esme Foster was his child? What would he do then?

Tess's singing faded and the hotel suite fell silent. Stefano stared at the cold glow of his laptop, wishing Tess would come out to talk to him.

He took a blanket and pillow from the closet and went back to the sofa. He stopped when he realized he'd forgotten to get pajamas. He didn't want to go to the bedroom and risk waking her, but he could hardly sleep naked, either, with her here.

He compromised by taking off only his shirt. He stretched out on the sofa beneath the blanket. He folded his hands on the pillow, behind his head, and stared at the ceiling, his jaw set.

His life didn't need to change, he told himself. He could simply tell his lawyers to arrange a generous financial settlement for Tess and the baby, and he could fly off to London as planned.

Tess was obviously a good mother. He could trust her to take care of Esme. Once they had unlimited money, they'd be fine. Tess would be free to do whatever she wanted. They didn't need Stefano.

Still, Stefano tossed and turned, remembering how alone he'd felt as a child, abandoned by his parents. Would Esme always think her father had deliberately chosen to abandon her? And if she did, wasn't it true?

Stefano woke from an unsettling dream to hear his phone ringing. He wrenched it to his ear. "Hello."

"It's Dr. Miller. I hope I didn't wake you. You said you wanted to know as soon as possible."

Looking out the windows, Stefano saw the light of early dawn. He gripped his phone. "Yes?"

"Esme Foster is your daughter. There can be no doubt."

Stefano closed his eyes. Part of him had already known—from the moment he'd really looked into the baby's dark eyes, exactly like his own.

You're Esme's father, Tess had said. *I have no reason to wait all night to get the news. I've waited for you long enough.*

"Your Highness?" the doctor said.

"Thank you," Stefano said flatly. "Send me your bill." He hung up.

Blinking, he sat up on the sofa, staring at the gray dawn over New York City, at the fine mist of September drizzle. Rising to his feet, he rolled his tense shoulders. He quietly went into the bedroom, careful not to wake Tess, who was sleeping half-upright, with their baby cuddled on her chest.

After taking clean clothes from the wardrobe, he went into the en suite bathroom. He closed and locked the door behind him, and took a shower so hot it scalded his skin. He shaved. He brushed his teeth. He wiped the steam off the mirror. He met his own eyes.

Nothing had to change, he repeated to himself. Nothing at all. He could still leave for London today. Let his lawyers handle this. He could continue to live his life as always.

A life of power and money.

Where he risked nothing.

Felt nothing.

Stefano's expression in the reflection was emotionless and cold. It was a trick he'd perfected long ago, imitating his father.

Once he was dressed in a crisp white shirt, dark trousers and a dark jacket, he went back into his bedroom. Reaching out, he gently shook Tess's shoulder.

Her eyes flew open, startled. When she saw him, standing over her in the shadows beside the bed, for a moment, she smiled in pure joy, as if all her dreams had come true.

Then she blinked, remembered and looked sad.

"What is it?" she said.

"The baby's mine."

She gave him a wistful smile. "I know." She waited, with painful hope in her eyes.

For what? What was Tess hoping? That he could settle down? Marry her? Help her raise the baby? Give them a home? A name?

Ridiculous.

Stefano had no idea how to be a good husband or father. He'd never even seen it done. Money was all he had to offer them. He'd give Tess a fortune and set her free.

But his body was fighting that decision. Even now, desire shuddered through him as he looked at her. She'd just woken up, but even in her rumpled clothes, tired and cuddling their sleeping baby in her arms, she was the most tantalizing woman he'd ever known.

What would it be like to wake up with her every morning? To have her in his bed every night? What would it be like to possess her completely?

Stefano pushed the thought aside savagely. Setting them free was the right thing to do. It would give Tess and their daughter the chance to be cherished and loved. By someone else.

And Stefano—

He'd focus on his upcoming negotiations. As Tess had said earlier, it was unacceptable that Stefano no longer even owned the corporate rights to his own name. He'd focus on that. Only on that.

And that was final.

"Come on, Tess," he said roughly, turning away. "I'll take you home."

CHAPTER THREE

TESS COULDN'T BELIEVE IT.

She glanced at Stefano out of the corner of her eye. They were sitting in the back seat of his expensive Rolls-Royce, with their baby in a car seat between them, as his uniformed driver maneuvered the morning rush-hour traffic already clogging the streets and avenues of New York in every direction.

She'd thought—really thought—that once he had proof he was Esme's father that he would offer to help her *somehow*. Hadn't he said that if he was the father, it would change everything?

Instead, he was taking her and Esme back to Brooklyn, to drop her off at her uncle's bakery on his way to the airport. Leaving Tess to face her uncle's wrath alone, while he flew off to London as planned.

Stefano had changed nothing.

Her disillusionment was complete.

"You're very quiet," Stefano said.

She couldn't even talk to him right now. Leaning forward, she spoke to the driver. "Thanks for the ride. I can't even imagine what it's like to drive in Manhattan."

"You don't know how to drive?" Stefano said.

She shook her head, still not looking at him. "I'm a New York girl. I take the subway."

But, as she spoke, her hand unconsciously stroked the smooth leather of the seat. It was a strangely sensual experience. But she'd only been in a luxury car like this once before. The night he'd seduced her. The night she'd conceived Esme.

"Ba-ba-ba," the baby said wonderingly beside her, waving her fat arms. Tess looked down at Esme with a tender smile.

"Yes. Exactly."

After Stefano had woken her up that morning, she'd fed and changed Esme, and brushed her own hair and teeth. A chauffeured Rolls-Royce had been waiting at the curb as they'd come out the front door of the Campania Hotel, and she'd found a brand-new infant car seat had already been installed in the back seat.

This must be what it's like to be rich, Tess thought. Your path through life was always smooth, because paid employees ran ahead of you, clearing and tidying up every problem or delay. Even a child was no problem, apparently. You could just drop her off with a clear conscience and fly away on your jet.

"You're angry with me," Stefano said quietly.

As they traveled over the Brooklyn Bridge, Tess

looked at him and immediately regretted it. "Why would I be angry?"

His eyes were dark and serious. "It's better this way."

"Better for who?"

"For you." He looked at the happy, gurgling baby. "For her."

Tess forced herself to smile. "You're probably right."

This would probably be the last time she'd ever see him, she realized. Stefano had made that clear since he'd woken her up and told her coldly that Esme was definitely his child, which, duh, she'd already known. What she'd hadn't known, what she'd waited with painful hope to hear, was how he would react to the news.

But all he'd said was that he was taking her home. After that, he'd avoided looking at her while the hotel staff had brought down his luggage from his suite.

Which was its own answer, really. Even now that Stefano had proof that Esme was his child, in spite of his earlier words, he didn't actually intend to do anything about it.

Tess was on her own.

It was a bitter pill to swallow. For over a year, she'd dreamed of Stefano returning to claim her, taking her in his arms, kissing her, begging her to be his bride. She'd dreamed of taking only one lover her whole life, and loving him for a lifetime. Being a family.

From the moment she'd met him on the street yesterday, she'd been forced to accept that, though Stefano Zacco might be a prince, he wasn't anything like the Prince Charming she'd imagined him to be. Still, part of her, deep inside, had hoped that once he knew without a doubt that Esme was his child, he'd change.

She was so stupid. Why did she always seek hope even at times she should have clearly accepted defeat?

"I want only the best for you both," Stefano said now. His black eyes pierced her heart.

His every action proved those words a lie. Taking a deep breath, she looked out at the passing buildings and said in a small voice, "So you're off to London now?"

"Yes. To negotiate for Zacco."

Her voice trembled a little as she said, "Good luck."

"Grazie," he said flatly.

They made their way through the most fashionable section of Brooklyn, toward the slightly less upscale neighborhood where her uncle's bakery had been started by his grandfather in 1940. Heads on the sidewalks turned as the gleaming car passed by.

She felt a hollow pang in her belly as she whispered, "My uncle is going to be furious because I was out all night…"

"Why do you care? You are only here to collect your things, and the baby's."

Frowning, Tess looked at him. "What are you talking about?"

Stefano snorted. "Surely you cannot wish to remain here, working yourself to exhaustion for little pay."

What choice do I have? She bit back the bitter words. She wouldn't let Stefano think she was asking for his money or anything else not freely given.

She was being foolish, she knew. Her practical, financially focused friend Lola would be screaming at her right now to demand a hefty dose of child support, as was her right, and as he could easily afford.

But she couldn't do it.

Tess had once wondered how her friend Hallie could have ever refused money from Cristiano Moretti under similar circumstances. Now, for the first time, she understood. It was because, after losing so much, sometimes a woman had only her pride left to cling to.

She set her jaw. "We'll be fine."

"Yes, I know. I've already called my lawyer."

Confused, she turned to him. "A lawyer? Why?"

"Now that I have proof of Esme's paternity, I cannot evade responsibility."

She sucked in her breath. "What do you mean?"

"Tess." Stefano's dark eyes glittered in the gray morning light. "Did you really think I'd leave you and Esme without a penny? My driver will return later this morning to collect you and Esme, and take you to my lawyer's office in Midtown. He'll arrange for your bank account and funds to buy a nice apartment in any neighborhood you desire. My driver will be at your disposal anytime, day or night. All your needs will be provided for, anything you need to make your life more comfortable. A housekeeper, a cook, charge accounts at every department store, private school for Esme."

Tess's mouth was open. "What?"

Stefano gave a hard, careless smile. "Why does this surprise you? It is now my duty to provide for you. You will never have to work again, Tess. Or do anything you do not wish to do."

Behind him, dimly Tess could see the Brooklyn Bridge and Manhattan skyline across the East River as the Rolls-Royce turned into her neighborhood.

When he'd said he wanted to take responsibility, for a moment she'd actually thought he intended to help raise their child, to be a real father; instead, he just meant money.

She should have been thrilled by his offer. Lola would have told her so in no uncertain terms. But she wasn't. Stefano made her feel as if she and

Esme were merely another unpleasant obligation, like an electricity bill.

Sadness filled her heart. Her shoulders sagged as she turned away, staring out at the Brooklyn street. Her street.

"Tess?"

As they pulled up in front of the bakery, she said in a low voice, "I don't want your money."

"Don't be ridiculous. It's all arranged. Watson will be back in about two hours, won't you, Watson?"

"Maybe three, depending on the traffic, Your Highness."

Stefano reached over the baby's car seat to take Tess's hand in his own. "You're free," he said in a low voice. "You and the baby can enjoy your lives." He paused. "Someday you'll find a man who deserves you both."

"Thanks," she said over the lump in her throat, pulling her hand away. His patronizing words burned her to the core. She would have preferred it if he'd told her that he found her boring and that he'd rather eat glass than raise a child. At least then she could have respected his honesty. Instead, he was trying to make it sound like he was abandoning Tess for *her* sake, which shamed her. "I guess this is goodbye, then." She tried to toss her head, to smile. "And good riddance, right?"

"What does that mean?"

"A man like you would never want to commit to a family. Especially not a family like us." Avoiding his eyes, she unbuckled Esme and lifted her into her arms, along with the diaper bag. Getting out of the back seat of the Rolls-Royce, she looked back at Stefano, so thuggishly handsome in his well-cut suit. The man she'd loved with such fierce, unwavering loyalty for so long.

That man had never truly existed. He was a man she'd made up in her own heart, someone noble and strong who just happened to have Stefano's face and voice.

Looking one last time into his dark eyes, she whispered, "Goodbye, Stefano."

She closed the car door firmly, shutting the door on her heart's fairy-tale dreams.

"Here you go, miss." The chauffeur set down her beat-up old stroller from the trunk, opening it for her on the sidewalk. "I'll return to Brooklyn for you and Miss Esme shortly."

"Thank you," she said, proud of herself for keeping her voice steady. As she settled her baby in the stroller, two young men passed by on the sidewalk, smiling at her. She vaguely recognized them as customers from the neighborhood and tried to smile back at them, but she couldn't manage it. Her heart was too sad. Squaring her shoulders, she looked ahead.

Foster Bros. Bakery, the sign proclaimed in

neon, over the faded paint of a sign original to 1940. The bakery had been expanded in the 1970s, and the window display now showed artificial wedding cakes with old, cracked white frosting over foam foundations. With a deep breath, Tess pushed open the door, causing the bell to chime.

Inside, the tables scattered across the rose-colored tile floor were far emptier than usual. There was only one customer, a white-haired poorly dressed regular named Peg, who came in each morning and paid for her coffee with nickels and dimes, then sat invisibly in the corner for hours, drinking coffee refills and reading newspapers other customers left behind.

Uncle Ray's head popped up over the bakery case.

"Where have you been?" he demanded as Tess came forward with the stroller. "Your aunt was so worried. We woke up this morning and had no idea where you were. Do you know how many messages we've left on your phone? She was about to call the police. The hospital. The morgue!"

Tess hung her head. "I'm sorry, Uncle Ray. I should have called."

He glared at her. "You shouldn't have stayed out all night! And with Esme, too." He looked down at the baby with a frown. "You should be ashamed, Tess. And since you weren't here to bake this morning, we have no pastries. Dozens of people walked out after they saw I had almost nothing to sell!"

The glass bakery case was indeed mostly empty, without Tess's pumpkin and maple scones, or pecan rolls or cherry Danish twists. The only pastry on offer was her aunt's morning glory super-bran honey-sweetened, carrot-and-zucchini muffin, which was a little too healthy for most.

"You could have asked Emily or Natalie. They're amazing bakers and—"

"They needed their sleep. They have class. I can't let them lose their only chance of college." *Not like you did*, his eyes seemed to say.

Tess's cheeks went hot. But she couldn't blame him for being upset. This bakery had been handed down from father to son for generations. Her uncle took it seriously.

After Tess's mother died when Tess was twelve, her aunt and uncle had brought her here to live with them. Tess had often puzzled over her uncle's appearance. He didn't look like bakers should look. Bakers were supposed to be fat and jolly, spreading joy to the world with cake and bread. Instead, Raymond Foster had the ascetic look of a marathon runner, spare and muscular, with a gaunt face and the downturned mouth of someone disappointed with his life. And now, because of her, he was even more disappointed.

Tess's shoulders slumped. "I'll go back and start baking, Uncle Ray."

"It's too late for pastries," her uncle barked. "Make cookies. Maybe we can sell them at lunch and after school."

"All right." Biting her lip, she paused. "Last night…it's not what you think. There was a good reason I didn't come home. I… I saw Esme's father."

Her uncle's eyes widened. "You did?"

She nodded.

Uncle Ray looked around. "So where is he?"

She swallowed. "He had to leave for London."

"Ah." Her uncle's eyes narrowed. "Right."

"I did see him! I did!" she said, hating the pleading sound of her own voice.

Her uncle sighed. "Then he obviously wants no part of you or Esme," he said quietly. "It's time to move on."

"He did offer to—"

"Enough, Tess. These romantic fantasies have ruined your life for long enough. I won't let them ruin our family's business, too."

She flinched, even knowing he was right. Stefano hadn't wanted any part of her or Esme. He hadn't even asked about seeing his daughter again. All he'd wanted to do was pay them off. To make them disappear. While she…

She wanted a father for her daughter. She

wanted a real home. She wanted a partner she could trust, someone she could share her life with. She'd wanted them to be a family.

Forget it, she told herself harshly. Her uncle was right. Romantic fantasies had ruined her life for long enough—

The bell chimed behind her. The bakery's door opened, and the cool September wind blew in. She heard a heavy step against the tile floor.

Maybe it was the faint scent of his cologne. The sound of his step.

But without even turning around, Tess sucked in her breath as prickles went up and down her body.

Her uncle's expression changed into a beaming smile as he looked past Tess to the new customer. "Yes, sir? How can I help you? We're out of pastries this morning, I'm afraid, but we have coffee and some very healthy muffins... How can I help you?"

"You can't." Stefano's voice was a growl. She closed her eyes, shivering. Coming directly behind her, he said in a low voice, "Tess. Look at me."

Slowly she turned.

Stefano looked like a dream to her, the handsome Sicilian prince staring down at her so hungrily, his muscular body powerful in a sleek designer suit.

"I thought you were leaving for London," she said, her voice trembling in spite of her best efforts.

"I am. But I forgot something."

"What?"

His sensual lips curved. "You."

"Me?" Tess whispered.

From the corner of her eye, she saw her uncle Ray's jaw drop.

Stefano put his hand on her cheek. "I can't leave you. I tried. I can't."

Electricity pulsed through her body at his touch. She breathed, "It seemed easy enough for you a minute ago."

He eyed the baby in the stroller, who looked back at him with dark eyes exactly like his own. He said simply, "I need you and Esme with me."

"In London?"

Leaning forward, he whispered, "Everywhere."

She felt the warmth of his breath against her skin, and her heartbeat quickened. For so long, Tess would have done anything to hear Stefano speak those words.

But she'd suffered too much shock and grief today. He couldn't tempt her to forget so easily how badly he'd treated her. She pulled away.

"Why would I come with you?"

Stefano's eyes widened. She saw she'd surprised him. And he wasn't the only one. Her uncle and the white-haired customer were now staring at them, wide-eyed.

Giving her a crooked grin, he said, "I can think of a few reasons."

"If you want to spend time with Esme, I will be happy to arrange that. But if you think I'll give up my family and friends and home—" she lifted her chin "—and come with you to Europe as some kind of paid nanny—"

"No. Not my nanny." Stefano's thumb lightly traced her tender lower lip. "I have something else in mind."

Unwilling desire shot down her body, making her nipples taut as tension coiled low in her belly. Her pride was screaming for her to push him away but it was difficult to hear her pride over the rising pleas of her body.

"I—I won't be your mistress, either," she stammered, shivering, searching his gaze.

"No." With a smile that made his dark eyes gleam, Stefano shook his head. "Not my mistress."

Tess heard a gasp. Glancing back at the cash register, she saw that her aunt and cousins had come downstairs from the upstairs apartment. They were standing next to her uncle, wearing the same stunned expressions.

"Then…then what?" Tess stammered, feeling foolish for even suggesting a handsome billionaire prince like Stefano would want a regular girl like her as his mistress. Her cheeks were hot. "You don't want me as your nanny, not as your mistress, so—what? You just want me to come to London as someone who watches your baby for free?" Her voice shook. "Some kind of…p-poor relation?"

"No." Taking her in his arms, Stefano said quietly, "Tess. Look at me."

Although she didn't want to obey, she could not resist. She opened her eyes, and the intensity of his glittering eyes scared her.

"I don't want you to be my mistress, Tess. I don't want you to be my nanny." His dark eyes burned through her. "I want you to be my wife."

Tess's beautiful face looked pale against her scarlet-red hair as she stood in the faded bakery. Her green eyes were shocked, even horrified.

Stefano was a little shocked himself. He marveled at how quickly everything had changed. Yesterday, before he'd known about the baby, marriage had been the last thing on his mind.

His own parents had hardly made him think well of the institution, and none of the ice-cold heiresses and greedy, pouting models Stefano had dated had ever tempted him to change his mind. Taking them to bed was more than enough.

Even an hour ago, knowing that Esme was his child, he'd grimly intended to let Tess go, leaving just his money to sustain them.

But when he'd watched Tess put their baby in a stroller and leave him, walking toward the bakery, he'd felt a jolt like a cold knife slicing through his solar plexus.

He hadn't wanted her to go.

Then he'd seen two men pass her on the sidewalk, slowing their walk to smile at her. Farther down the street, they'd turned back to look at her again. Their polite smiles changed to leers as they elbowed each other. Stefano could only imagine what the two men were saying about her. Or what they'd like to do to her.

The knife in Stefano's gut had twisted deeper. He didn't want to imagine Tess with another man. Ever. And yet he'd let her go so she could find a man who could love her. A better man.

But what if the next man wasn't better?

What if he was worse?

Admittedly love was a mysterious emotion to Stefano, as he'd never experienced it. From the outside, it seemed like a self-inflicted delusion, an addictive madness that people used as an excuse to behave badly. Love came like a hurricane and left like a tornado, leaving people trampled and homes destroyed.

It had been that way with his parents, and to an entire army of their discarded lovers and spouses, in their exhaustive quest for love. And all the while, they'd left their only child to languish in an isolated castle in the care of paid servants. To them, children were an unacceptable impediment to enjoying a love affair.

What if the man Tess chose was similarly self-ish and cruel? What if he treated her badly? What if he cheated on her? Stole from her? Hit her?

What if, far from him being a better father than Stefano, he resented raising another man's child and mistreated Esme? What if he abused her?

A cold shudder had gone down Stefano's spine.

He'd thought giving up Tess and the baby was the right thing to do—for their sakes. In that moment, however, he'd suddenly realized he was leaving them to the mercy of wolves. And Tess, with her kind nature and optimistic heart, might not know the difference until it was too late.

After all, she'd thought Stefano was worth a year of total loyalty. How badly astray could those rose-colored glasses lead her?

There was only one way to be permanently sure of their security. One way to keep them safe.

He had to marry her.

Perhaps Stefano couldn't love her. Even so, he could damn sure take care of her. And his child.

As he'd sat in the back seat of the Rolls-Royce, the desire—the need—to permanently claim Tess as his own had rushed through him with the force of a tidal wave. When she had disappeared into the bakery, his driver had started to pull away from the curb.

"Stop!" Stefano had shouted.

He'd couldn't let her go. He couldn't let them both disappear and trust that the next man would deserve Tess more than he did. He'd thought he could.

He was wrong.

Now Stefano looked down at her in the bakery's soft light. He was dimly aware of some old love song playing on the radio. From behind the counter, four people, a man and woman and two teenaged girls with backpacks, watched with their mouths wide. Ah, yes, Stefano thought. That must be the aunt and uncle and cousins who'd made Tess speak with such fear about being a *poor relation*. Stefano could hardly wait to take her away from the bakery and treat her as she deserved—like a princess.

"Well?" he said gently. "What is your answer?"

She shifted her feet uncertainly on the tile floor. "You—you want to marry me?"

"Yes."

"You can't mean it," she choked out, searching his gaze desperately. "A man like you could never be faithful to just one woman."

"You're wrong," he said flatly. "I've seen the damage of that in my parents' marriage. I would never betray you."

Tess bit her lip, looking up at him.

"Say yes, dearie!" cried the bakery's only customer, an elderly woman nursing a coffee at the furthest table. "He's a hunk!"

"I…" Tess looked down. Her dark eyelashes swept against the smattering of freckles on her pale cheeks. "I don't understand. The only good reason to marry," she said in a small voice, "is for love."

"You once said you loved me," he pointed out.

Her lips curved. "As you pointed out, that was before I even knew you."

The edges of his lips quirked. "So, get to know me."

Her eyes widened, then she shook her head, repeating stubbornly, "Love is the only reason for marriage."

Stefano thought about arguing with her, of pointing out that, in his opinion, romantic love was at best a biological reaction brought on by hormones and pheromones to coax a couple into settling into domestic life; at worst it was a delusion, an intoxicating dream that people used like a drug to escape real life. But with Tess's romantic heart, suddenly he knew all rational arguments would be wasted. Only an emotional appeal would work.

Deliberately, he lowered his head so his lips nearly brushed against her ear. He felt her shiver as he breathed in the scent of her red hair, like vanilla and flowers.

"You are the only woman I've ever wanted to be my wife. Only you."

He felt her shiver as she pulled away. Her emerald eyes were almost pleading. "But…"

He cupped her cheek. "I can make you and Esme happy," he said softly. "You'll always be protected and safe. We'll travel the world by private jet. You'll have homes in Paris and Rome and St. Barts. A castle in Sicily."

Her lips parted. "You have a *castle*?"

"It's a bit of a ruin." He gave her a wickedly seductive smile. "But yes."

"A castle," she whispered to herself.

Still, Tess didn't say yes. Other women might have been lured with dreams of wealth and status—not her.

Stefano took a different tack.

"You had to drop out of design school," he murmured, twisting a tendril of her red hair around his finger. "As my wife, you'll be far more influential in the fashion world than any mere designer. You'll be invited to every event. Runway shows. Fashion awards. Berlin. The Met Gala."

"I will?" she breathed.

He drew her closer into his arms, not caring who saw. Even baby Esme seemed almost solemn, watching from the stroller.

"Let me make you a princess." His hand gently stroked down her cheek to the edge of her throat, to her shoulder. His gaze fell to her pink lips as he whispered, "Let me give you the fairy tale."

Tess's eyes were huge. He could see she was tempted. But, still, she didn't say yes.

Why?

He thought of everything he'd ever done to persuade a woman into his bed. He'd never imagined, he thought with grim amusement, that he'd someday need even greater charm to persuade a woman to *wed*.

What else could he offer, aside from the heart he did not have? What could he propose that wasn't a lie?

Then he remembered what Tess cared about most.

"Let me give our daughter a name," he said huskily. "Let me give her a home. Let me be her father. I want you as my wife. My family."

Pulling the solid gold signet ring off his finger, Stefano slowly went down on one knee. All the women in the bakery gasped, but he had eyes only for her. He took her hand, looking up at her.

"Marry me, Tess."

She sucked in her breath. He saw tears in her eyes, and he knew he had her.

"Until I can get you a diamond ring, I offer this." He held up the signet ring. "It's been in my family for generations. I give it as my pledge of fidelity. My promise of forever." He looked up at her. "Will you, Tess? Will you be mine, not just now, but forever?"

For a moment, she seemed to hold her breath, as if caught between desire and fear.

"Say yes," squealed one of her young cousins.

"Yes!" cried the other one.

"Do it, Tess," her aunt said hoarsely. "Seize your dreams before it's too late."

The uncle was silent, watching them.

Tess shivered. Then her fingers tightened over his.

"Yes," she whispered.

Triumph rushed through Stefano, greater than he'd ever felt before, even when he'd made his first million, when he'd made his first *billion*. This was better. What he'd assumed was an entitlement to be merely demanded—Tess's hand in marriage—had become, with her hesitation, a prize to be fought for and won.

Still kneeling, he fervently kissed her hand, then slid on the gold signet ring engraved with the Zacco coat of arms. Her fingers were too delicate, so it would fit only on her thumb, and even then, she had to keep her hand closed.

"We'll get you another ring immediately," he promised, rising to his feet. But he didn't release her hand. He loved the feel of her smaller hand in his own, and soon he would have more of her.

All of her.

Tess gave him a shy smile. "I like your ring fine."

"Plain gold? No. You'll have a diamond. The best in the city." Only one woman in a million, he thought, would have said she didn't need a big diamond ring. Only one woman would have been reluctant to marry him unless it was for the right reasons. A woman who put her child above herself, and who was loyal and kind and true.

As he stood beside her in the weak September light from the bakery's windows, her family rushed forward to congratulate them. Stefano looked at Tess, now being hugged tearfully by her aunt and cousins.

He could hardly wait to marry her.

"You'd better take good care of her," the uncle said gruffly behind him. "After the year of hell you put her through."

Stefano turned with a single brusque nod. "I will."

"When will you marry?" the aunt asked, smiling.

He turned to Tess. "Tomorrow."

They all looked at one another, astonished. "Tomorrow?"

"Yes. I'll take you to London as my wife."

Her beautiful face appeared entranced as she nodded, ducking her head. "All right," she whispered. "Tomorrow."

"I cannot wait," he said huskily, feeling a swell of pride and the glory of conquest. Cupping her face in his hands, he lowered his mouth passionately to hers. Tomorrow couldn't come soon enough.

CHAPTER FOUR

"ARE YOU SURE about this, Tess?"

Tess looked up in surprise. She was wearing a wedding dress, sitting in a chair in an elegant private sitting room of the Campania Hotel, getting the final touches of her makeup done by a stylist. Doubt was the last thing she'd ever expected from *Lola*, of all people. Especially now, just minutes before the wedding ceremony was set to begin!

"Of course I'm sure," Tess said uneasily. "Why wouldn't I want to marry Stefano? He's Esme's father!"

Lola lifted a skeptical eyebrow. "I didn't hear you say anything about love."

"Of course Tess loves him," Hallie protested, sipping a mimosa nearby. "She's loved him for a year. Even when we teased her about it!"

"Yeah, I know. We thought you were crazy." Lola's eyes challenged Tess in the mirror. "So he's everything you imagined him to be?"

Tess's cheeks burned. "Pretty much."

"He told you he loves you?"

Tess bit her lip. "Um…"

"Has he or hasn't he?"

Looking between them, the stylist packed up her gear and excused herself, closing the door of the sitting room quietly behind her. With a deep breath, Tess looked at her two friends.

Lola and Hallie were wearing bridesmaid dresses in her favorite color, emerald green. Their three babies were already in the grand ballroom with Tess's cousins and Hallie's husband, Cristiano. The wedding was set to begin in minutes. Any moment now, the Campania's wedding planner would burst in with her headset and clipboard to tell them it was time for the whirlwind ceremony to begin.

Tess said slowly, "I've realized we don't really know each other that well. But we have a child now, so I...hope love will come in time."

Hallie and Lola glanced at each other uneasily.

"He hasn't told you he loves you?" Hallie said. "And now you're saying you don't love him?"

Turning in the chair, Tess glared at her friends.

"How long did it take for Cristiano to tell you he loved you, Hallie?" The brunette hung her head in answer. "And you." Tess narrowed her eyes at Lola. "Aren't you the one who's always going on about how mothers have an obligation to be financially stable for their children?"

"That *is* what you always say, Lola," Hallie said.

"But you're not like me, Tess," she said. "You don't care about money. You just want to be loved."

Tess felt a sharp pain in her throat.

"I want you to be careful, that's all. Don't do anything you'll regret." The blonde looked away. "Don't love him if you know he'll never love you back."

"Is that what happened to you, Lola?" Tess said timidly. "You've never said what happened with Jett's father…"

"We're talking about you, not me." She looked down. Her voice became sad. "I don't want to see you make a mistake, that's all."

Tess and Hallie looked at each other. This wasn't like their brash friend. Usually Lola couldn't wait to boss them around. *Speaking the brutal truth with love*, Lola called it, although her words were sometimes far more brutal than loving.

But then Lola hadn't seemed quite herself lately. No wonder, Tess thought. Lola had a newborn. That kind of exhaustion would put any woman off her game.

Tess hadn't slept very well last night, either. Knowing it was her last evening in her aunt and uncle's Brooklyn apartment, she'd stared up at the shadowy ceiling, tormented by anxiety. Without Stefano's overwhelming presence to reassure her, she'd felt a strange fear over this sudden marriage.

It's just cold feet, she'd tried to tell herself then. But now she wondered—what if it wasn't?

She'd never thought getting married would scare

her. She'd always been sure that when she wed, she'd be so deeply in love she'd rush into the ceremony with a pure, joyful heart.

Today she was marrying a man she barely knew. Not for love, but because they had a child.

Maybe Stefano *could* love me, she told herself desperately. Someday. And if he did, who knew? Maybe she could someday be brave enough to forget how he'd hurt her. Maybe she could be brave enough to open up her heart again, too.

But was she willing to take the gamble? Because if Stefano couldn't love her, why would she be stupid enough to open herself up to more heartbreak? She wouldn't. Lola was right. She could never let herself love Stefano again, even if she wanted to. Not unless he loved her first.

But what if he didn't? Could she live her whole life without love?

Tess glanced at the empty champagne glasses on the table, next to the bouquets made by the hotel florist. Yesterday she'd relished her friends' shock and delight when she'd told them that her baby's long-lost father had returned, revealing himself to be a billionaire prince. And, not only that, he wished to marry Tess immediately!

Lola and Hallie's giddy squeals had been music to Tess's ears. She'd loved showing off the sparkling ten-carat diamond engagement ring Stefano had bought her on Fifth Avenue, after they'd left

City Hall with their marriage license. She was wearing the diamond ring now, and though part of her already missed the simple integrity of Stefano's gold signet ring, obviously she couldn't go around wearing it on her thumb. She'd told herself she'd get used to the cold weight of the diamond in time.

Getting ready for the wedding with her two best friends had seemed like a good idea. And at first it had been wonderful. They'd giggled, drinking mimosas, and Tess had felt contented.

But now the gorgeous platinum-set ten-carat diamond ring hung heavily on Tess's left hand.

Shaking, she rose to her feet.

"Fine bridesmaids you two make," she said accusingly, "trying to talk me into jilting him at the last minute."

The other two hung their heads.

"Sorry, Tess," Hallie said. "He is your baby's father, after all."

"Sorry," Lola muttered.

Tess lifted her chin. "I never had a father or a real home. Don't you think I want that for Esme?"

"Of course you do," Hallie said soothingly.

"I'm sure you'll be very happy." But Lola didn't sound sure at all.

Tess swallowed. "Stefano has promised to be faithful. All he wants is to make me happy." Her voice trembled. "He's going to whisk me away to London and Milan and Paris for our honeymoon—"

"Some honeymoon." Lola snorted. "A fashion CEO dragging you to all the Fashion Weeks. That's not a honeymoon—it's a business trip!"

"I studied fashion design," Tess said defensively. "I can't wait to be a part of it!"

"Sure, as his trophy wife. Not a designer."

Tears rose to Tess's eyes.

"You hush," Hallie told Lola harshly. "Don't listen to her," she said, patting Tess's hand.

"I'm just trying to save you from a lot of grief," Lola said flatly. "The fact that he's a billionaire only makes it worse. Because billionaires don't know how to love anyone." Her eyes were bleak. "I know."

"Excuse *me*," Hallie said.

"Except your husband, Hallie. He's one in a million." Lola's face gentled into a smile. Then she shook her head. "Doesn't Cristiano have anything to say about this wedding? He hates Stefano Zacco!"

Hallie shrugged. "Cristiano says since Tess has a child with Stefano, she must see something good in him, and on her own head be it." She grinned. "I think my husband must be remembering that I didn't always think so highly of *him*, either."

Slowly Lola picked up her bridesmaid's bouquet

in a rustle of rose petals. "I think it's a mistake to leave your family and friends, and get married after a one-day engagement to a man you barely know." Wiping her eyes, she tried to smile. "But, of all people, you deserve the fairy tale, Tess. If you're sure Stefano's the one, then I wish you every happiness. I…" Her voice broke. "I'll see you in there."

The blonde hurried out of the room.

"She's just worried about you," Hallie said.

Tess looked at herself in the full-length mirror. Stefano had arranged for one of his smaller luxury fashion brands, Fontana, to make her a lavish wedding dress. The gown was exquisite, made of white satin, with full skirts and a corset bodice with a sweetheart neckline. The edges were embroidered with tiny diamonds, and so was the long white veil that trailed down her back, over her red hair that was pulled back into a chignon. Anchoring the veil was a 300-year-old diamond tiara, an heirloom of the Zacco family.

Her green eyes were lined with black kohl and mascara, her lips ruby red with lipstick. As Tess looked at herself in the mirror, she barely recognized herself. But in spite of the gown, the veil and the tiara, she suddenly thought she didn't look right for a bride. There wasn't any joy in her expression. Her eyes were scared.

"This is your life, and Esme's," Hallie said quietly, handing Tess her bridal bouquet of pink roses. "Trust your heart. It will tell you what's right."

Slowly taking her bouquet, Tess thought of how she'd felt when Stefano had pulled her into his arms in the bakery and demanded that she become his bride. Everyone had been so happy for her. In that moment, she'd felt like the luckiest girl on earth. Wasn't she?

And the decision was already made.

Wasn't it?

Taking a deep breath, Tess turned to Hallie. "Could you ask Stefano to come talk to me?"

"Right now?"

"Yes. Just for a moment, here in private?"

Hallie's eyes widened, then she said quietly, "Of course. I'll go get him. Then I'll wait in the hall for…for whatever you decide," she finished lamely. She left, closing the door softly behind her.

Tess looked out at the golden afternoon sunlight pouring through the window. Setting down her bouquet, she placed her hands against the corset boning of her gown's bodice, trying to make herself take long, slow breaths instead of panicked little gasps. Why was she suddenly so afraid?

Closing her eyes, Tess had the sudden memory of the day long ago when her mother had collapsed on their old shabby sofa, sobbing, unable to catch her breath.

"It's over," Serena Foster had choked out, whispering, "He's never coming back."

"Who?" Tess had asked anxiously. Just eight years old, she'd been alarmed to see her determinedly cheerful mother fall apart without warning.

Shaking her head, her mother had wiped her eyes and tried to smile. "It doesn't matter."

"Pinkie loves you, Mama," Tess had said desperately, pushing her ragged pink unicorn into her mother's arms. "And so do I."

"Thank you, darling." Hugging Tess fiercely, Serena had wiped her eyes. "I was stupid to love him. But he's a bigger fool by far…"

Tess opened her eyes when she heard a single knock at the door. It creaked half open.

"This is a bad idea," came Stefano's gravelly voice from the other side. "I don't generally care about wedding traditions, but even I know the groom isn't supposed to see the bride before the ceremony."

Her heart lifted at hearing his voice. She knew once they talked she'd feel better. "I don't care. Just come in. I need you."

Stefano peeked his head around the door, then came toward her in the hotel's luxurious private sitting room.

In his well-cut tuxedo, Stefano looked powerful, broad shouldered and devastatingly handsome. His dark eyes widened above his chiseled cheekbones when he saw Tess in her wedding gown. "You are so beautiful, *cara*." As he took her in his arms, the hard lines of his face glowed with fierce pride. "I can hardly wait to take you as my wife."

Taking a deep breath, she said timidly, "But you don't love me, do you?"

Stefano blinked, then pulled back, his forehead furrowed. "What?"

Nervously she licked her lips. "I'm just wondering if we're doing the right thing," she whispered, staring down at the elegant Turkish rug on the gleaming hardwood floor. "I mean, we don't love each other. I'm wondering…if someday you think we might… I'm just scared this whole thing might be a terrible mistake."

Her words seemed to echo against the walls. She waited desperately for him to kiss her, to reassure her. Instead, he said nothing. Finally she looked up.

Stefano's dark eyes were cold as ice. The expression on his handsome face chilled her to the bone.

"You wish to cancel the wedding?" he said softly. "To disgrace my name? To take my child away?"

What she'd wanted was reassurance. This was exactly the opposite. "All I want is for us to talk—"

"Is there another man?"

"No, of course not!"

"But you are having second thoughts." He gave

her a bitter smile. "Or is this a ploy to renegotiate the prenuptial agreement you signed yesterday?"

"No!" Why would she want to alter the prenup? She'd barely read it. She took a deep breath. "I'm afraid."

"And I am afraid," he said with dangerous silkiness, "that you already gave me your word. We have a verbal contract. It's done."

Tess herself had thought something similar just moments before—that the decision had already been made, so there was no backing out. But hearing him speak the words like a threat made her back stiffen. "What are you saying?"

His eyes narrowed.

"You're wearing my ring." He looked down at the big diamond on her left hand. "You will take my name. You will be my wife, and we will raise our daughter. Our wedding will go forward as planned."

She tried to toss her head, not easy when it was weighed down with a heavy diamond tiara. "Maybe I won't!"

His lips twisted. Reaching out, he cupped her cheek, running his thumb along her shaking lower lip.

"And maybe," he said tenderly, "I'll hire a team of lawyers to utterly destroy you and your family. Maybe I'll take our daughter and make sure you never see her again."

Then Stefano drew back, his dark eyes smiling down at her as if he'd been flirting.

The room, with all its elegant furnishings, seemed to spin around her. Tess stared up at him, her eyes wide with horror.

"Are you ready, Miss Foster?"

Tess turned to see the hotel's wedding planner with her headset standing in the doorway. Behind her, Uncle Ray hovered.

"Yes. She's ready." Stefano's eyes were callous as he looked down at Tess. "Aren't you?"

Feeling sick inside, she gave an unsteady nod.

"What are you doing here, Your Highness?" the wedding planner chided. "You're supposed to be waiting in the ballroom."

"Of course." Deliberately, Stefano reached down and pulled the translucent white veil over Tess's tiara, over her face. He said lightly, "I can't wait to marry you, *cara mia*."

And, after kissing her cheek through the veil, he left.

Tess stood in shock as her uncle came forward with tears in his eyes.

"You look beautiful, Tessie." He held out his arm awkwardly in the new designer tuxedo that Stefano had provided for him. "Are you ready for this?"

Numbly Tess took her uncle's arm. She picked up her bouquet.

"Thank you for walking me down the aisle, Uncle Ray," she said, barely knowing what she was saying. She felt frozen, like she was in a bad dream.

"My little sister would be so proud of you," her uncle said, blinking back tears. "Of the woman you've become."

"I wish Mama was still here," Tess whispered. After Tess's father had left, her mother had gone through many other short-lived romances—surely Serena would have known what to do now.

They followed the wedding planner down the elegant hallway, toward the entrance to the grand hotel ballroom, where her two bridesmaids waited outside the door. Lola refused to meet her eyes. Hallie took one look at Tess and demanded, "What's wrong?"

"Nothing," Tess said, looking away.

"Stefano just rushed by us. I guess that means you guys worked it out?" she said hopefully.

"You might say that," Tess said. *Maybe I'll take our daughter and make sure you never see her again.*

The double doors opened and a wave of music swelled as the orchestra started the first notes of the wedding march. Bouquets held high, Lola walked in, followed by Hallie.

"Here we go," her uncle whispered. Tess nodded, and clutching his arm like a life preserver, she walked forward.

Hundreds of guests rose to their feet in the gilded ballroom, beneath soaring ceilings and sparkling crystal chandeliers. Tess looked around desperately for a friendly face among the glamorous strangers staring at her incredulously, as if wondering why on earth a handsome billionaire prince would lower himself to marrying the likes of her.

They didn't know how much Tess desperately wished she wasn't marrying him now.

Lola had been right. Why, oh, why hadn't Tess gotten to know Stefano better before she'd agreed to be his wife? Why had she let herself get swept up in the romantic moment?

Why had she let her blindly, stupidly optimistic heart make the decision, instead of her brain?

Tess's knees shook. Looking through the crowd, she finally saw her own friends and family, who gave her encouraging smiles. Her aunt had tears in her eyes. She saw her cousin Natalie, holding Esme, whispering happily to the baby as she pointed at Tess. Nearby, friends from her neighborhood waved at her. Women she knew from the single moms support group she'd attended last year beamed at her as she walked by, including the woman who'd introduced her to Hallie and Lola. Lacey Tremaine Drakos stood with her ruggedly handsome Greek husband, holding their baby in her arms.

Then Tess looked forward, saw Stefano, and everything else faded to a blur.

He stood alone beside the minister, without a best man, in front of the guests, beneath a canopy of roses. His dark eyes gleamed down at her.

The bastard.

Tess's hands tightened on her bouquet. She would have dearly loved to smash his smug face with it.

As she reached the front, she barely heard the minister's words. "Who gives this woman to be married to this man?" Or her uncle's answer: "Her aunt and I do." She barely noticed the minister's long-winded advice on the duties of marriage. He might as well have been reading from a technical manual written in hieroglyphics.

As the minister spoke the words that would make them husband and wife, all of Tess's feelings and thoughts melted to one single overwhelming emotion for the man beside her.

Hate.

Stefano's expression was cool and impersonal. As their gaze locked and held, it changed. His eyes turned dark, hungry.

Tess was suddenly aware that they were flying like an out-of-control train toward the end of the ceremony, when Stefano would claim her as his wife and kiss her.

Then, tonight, on their wedding night, he would do far more than kiss her.

Tess's toes curled in her expensive white high heels. Out of pure hate, she told herself.

But the truth was more complicated. Even in her rage, as she watched the flick of his tongue against his cruel, sensual lips, her own lips tingled in response. Against her will, her whole body sizzled at his closeness, aching in its most secret places.

"And do you, Tesslyn Mae Foster, take this man to be your lawfully wedded husband?"

Gazing up at Stefano, Tess hesitated, heart pounding in her throat. She could refuse him now. In front of everyone. Tell him to go to hell. She *could.*

Stefano waited, his eyes narrowing. Three hundred guests held their breath.

I'll hire a team of lawyers to utterly destroy you and your family... I'll take our daughter and make sure you never see her again.

"I do," she ground out, furious and wretched.

"I now pronounce you husband and wife." The minister beamed at them. "You may kiss the bride."

Stefano lifted her long, translucent white veil off her face, back over the diamond tiara. Reaching down, he cupped her face with his hands.

Her knees went wobbly. Part of her wanted to turn away, to kick him in the shins. To scream in his face.

But not all of her. Part of her still wanted him. *Even now.* Heaven help her.

As Stefano pulled her into his arms, so close she

could almost hear the beat of his heart, she felt the warmth of his breath, sweet and spicy as cloves. She shivered, holding her breath, frozen beneath her tight bodice.

With agonizing slowness, he lowered his head. Then his lips touched hers, and electricity pulsed through her body. He deepened the kiss, twisting his tongue against hers, publicly claiming her as his possession. She gasped beneath the brutal onslaught of pleasure, and to her shame, a soft moan came from the back of her throat.

When he finally pulled away, applause mounted like a storm swell as guests rose to their feet with a cheer.

Stefano lowered his head, nuzzling her ear. He whispered huskily, "That was quite a kiss."

Tess stared at him, trembling between fury and desire. Fury won.

Smiling for the crowd, she ground out through her teeth, "I hope you enjoyed it. Because that's the last time I'll ever let you kiss me."

His eyes narrowed.

"Allow me to present," the minister cried, "Their Highnesses Prince Stefano and Princess Tess Zacco di Gioreale!"

Holding her hand tightly, Stefano turned and waved at his friends, smiling like a happy bridegroom.

Tess knew a storm was coming. She could feel

it building, like low-rolling thunder rattling toward them without mercy.

Her new husband intended to seduce her. To possess her. *She couldn't let him.*

It was all she could think about during the wedding reception immediately afterward in the grand ballroom. She felt the hum of her body's desire and grimly fought it, tooth and nail, until she nearly panted with exhaustion, even as she went through the motions of what was supposed to be the happiest day of her life.

Tess forced herself to smile until her cheeks ached as she accepted the congratulations of her family and friends. She held poses for endless wedding photographs. She mechanically ate an elegant dinner of salmon, baby potatoes and asparagus in a lemon-butter sauce, followed by wedding cake. She sipped champagne as toasts were offered by strangers.

She forced herself to make polite responses as Stefano introduced her to many fashion industry insiders, including the extremely thin, severely chic Fenella Montfort, whom he introduced as the majority shareholder of the Zacco brand. He'd added with a charming smile, "Though we'll talk more about that in London, won't we, Fenella?"

"If we must," the older woman said coolly.

As Tess's desire fought against her howling fury,

her mind scrambled for a way to escape this marriage. Could she go to Hallie and Cristiano for help? Ask them to assist her in filing for a divorce?

But even if Cristiano Moretti gave her all his man-eating lawyers, she knew that divorce would be an endless, bloody war, with Esme its greatest victim.

Lost in her own churning emotions, Tess barely noticed when, after she tossed the wedding bouquet and Lola accidentally caught it, the blonde turned pale and immediately dropped it to the floor. Lola practically ran out of the reception, pausing only to grab her baby's stroller as other female guests fought for the bouquet in a flurry of rose petals. Normally Tess would have been alarmed for her friend.

But not today. Today nothing could reach her through her own haze of rage and fear.

Until this.

The tradition of the groom pulling the garter off the bride's leg was supposed to be a harmless bit of fun, a sly nod to tradition to entertain wedding guests. Now, as Stefano knelt before Tess, who was seated in a chair, her heartbeat went to a thousand as he pushed up her full skirts. His dark eyes burned through hers as he slowly pulled the blue satin garter down her leg. His fingertips brushed against her bare skin.

Time slowed. She forgot her anger and fear. In

this moment, all she could see was the hunger in his eyes, pulling her down into the flames.

Though they were surrounded by hundreds of strangers, it was just the two of them. Alone.

When he finally turned away, to toss the garter into the crowd of eager single men, Tess rose abruptly to her feet with a strangled gasp. She muttered, "I have to check on Esme," and fled for the head table.

"I'll come with you," he replied.

As he followed her back to the table, Tess was careful not to let Stefano touch her, not even her hand.

When they reached the elaborate, flower-decorated table for the wedding party and close family, Tess was dismayed to find Esme sitting happily in her cousin Natalie's arms. If the baby had been fussy, it would have been an excellent excuse for Tess to take her and go.

But go where? She could hardly return to her aunt and uncle's apartment tonight. All of Tess and Esme's meager belongings had been packed in two shabby suitcases and were already upstairs in Stefano's hotel suite, where she was supposed to sleep tonight. Natalie had volunteered to babysit Esme until they collected her on their way to the airport in the morning.

"I can't believe you guys did it," Hallie said, sitting comfortably beside Cristiano at the table. She shook her head. "How on earth did you pull such a big wedding together in one day?"

"Ask Moretti," Stefano replied smoothly. Reaching for his flute, he took a sip of champagne. "All I did was tell him to arrange it."

"It wasn't difficult, Zacco," Cristiano said. "Not when the words you used were *make it happen at any price*." The hotel tycoon sat with one arm draped over his wife's shoulders, the other holding their adorable baby, Jack. He quirked an eyebrow. "There's nothing we enjoy more at the Campania than unreasonable requests, as long as money's no object. Even for a conniving bastard like you, Zacco."

"Conniving?" Stefano bared his teeth into a smile. "You are the one who tried to cheat, by blocking my car in the race." He shrugged. "If you wanted to win, you should have gone faster."

"You could have caused an accident."

"I knew you were a decent enough driver that you wouldn't let that happen. Decent." Stefano saluted him with his champagne flute. "Just slow."

With a snort, Cristiano shook his head. "There are more important things in life than winning some cheap gold trophy in a charity race." He stroked his wife's shoulder. "It's a foolish man who's determined to win at any price."

"So losers always say."

The two powerful men glowered at each other,

then suddenly they both laughed. Smiling, Hallie rose to her feet.

She looked at Tess. "It's time for your first dance as bride and groom, isn't it?"

The last thing Tess wanted to do right now was slow dance in her new husband's arms. Her cheeks went hot as she looked down at her clasped hands. "I think we've had enough traditions for one day…"

"Oh, please," Hallie begged. "I was planning to sing for your first dance. As a surprise."

Put that way, it seemed churlish to refuse.

"All right," Tess sighed. "Fine."

"Yay." Hallie looked down at her seated husband with a tender smile. "Wish me luck."

"You don't need it." Cristiano pulled her into his arms and lifted his lips to hers in a sensual kiss. "You'll knock 'em dead."

Watching the other couple, so deeply in love, Tess again felt a pang over what she now knew she would never have.

As Hallie hurried toward the microphone on the grand ballroom's stage, Stefano held out his hand.

"Shall we?" he said, smiling down at her as if he hadn't just blackmailed her into marriage and threatened to destroy her family and take her child away.

Glaring at him, Tess grudgingly put her hand in his and tried not to feel the electricity of his touch.

"And now," Hallie announced over the microphone, "for their very first dance, the Prince and Princess of Gioreale!"

A hush fell across the crowd as Stefano led her, in a swirl of her white satin skirts, onto the dance floor.

To the outside world, Tess knew it must look like a romantic moment, the handsome prince in his sleek, well-cut tuxedo, the bride in a lavish wedding gown sparkling with diamonds, dancing in his arms. The truth was anything but romantic.

The orchestra began playing the music of the song Tess had requested, one made famous by Etta James and that she'd loved since she was a child—"At Last." Hallie's beautiful voice started singing the haunting words, telling the rapturous tale of long-lost love finally requited.

Yesterday Tess had dreamily thought it was perfect. Now, in her husband's arms, all she felt was bitterness.

She looked up at his face.

"I hate you," she whispered. "You know that, don't you?"

Stefano looked down at her as they swayed, his handsome face arrogant. "You don't hate me. You're just angry. It will pass."

"Are you crazy? You forced me to marry you."

"I didn't force you. I offered you a choice."

"What—marry you or lose everything?"

His eyes gleamed in the spotlight as they danced to the music. "I knew you'd make the right decision."

Tess yearned to stomp hard on his foot with one of her stiletto heels. Instead, she bared her teeth into a smile for the benefit of the guests watching them as he whirled her around the dance floor.

"You are a monster," she said sweetly.

"Cheer up." He pulled her hard against his body. "I told you the truth. I intend to make you very happy in our marriage. Starting tonight."

He cupped her cheek, and desire crackled through her body, from her scalp to her toes and everywhere in between.

Breathing hard, she turned away.

"Go to hell," she spit out, trying to hide her conflicting feelings. How could her body still want him, when she despised him?

"I intend to satisfy you in every way possible." He stopped on the dance floor, looking down at her. "Tonight, you will be in my bed. Willingly and completely."

Trembling, she lifted her chin. In spite of her best efforts, her voice trembled as she taunted, "In your dreams."

"My dreams always come true." Stefano cupped her face in both his hands. "I always win, like Moretti said. I take what I want, at any price. And what I want—" he slowly lowered his mouth to hers "—is you."

Tess held her breath. She knew she should push him away, resist, but she couldn't. When his lips finally pressed against hers, the intoxication of his caress made her feel dizzy. She had to clutch his shoulders to keep from falling. The world spun around her as if she'd drunk far more than one glass of champagne.

Dimly she heard whistling and hooting from the crowd, but they all seemed far away. In Stefano's arms, swaying to this beautiful song she'd loved all her life, her anger faded for a moment and her old dream resurfaced in her heart. She'd yearned for him for so long. Her perfect man. Her handsome prince. Their kiss brought it all back, sending her soaring into the sky.

As the song ended, he pulled away and Tess slowly opened her eyes.

Stefano stared down at her, his dark eyes wide as if he'd felt the same shock, the two of them in their own private world.

Applause thundered around them—for their first dance as husband and wife, and for Hallie's amazing performance.

Stricken, Tess touched her bruised lips. How could she keep kissing him like that? With everything in her heart? Her body ached for him, and her nipples felt tight beneath the smooth silk bodice.

For over a year, she'd been tormented by hot,

sensual dreams of Stefano, of the night he'd taken her virginity and they'd conceived a child. She'd yearned for the man she'd imagined him to be. Now she knew the truth.

The dream still held sway over her.

She *wanted* to be in his bed. No matter how she tried to fight it. No matter how she pretended otherwise. Even now, looking up at him, she unconsciously licked her lips. She heard his soft groan and felt lost in his dark, hungry gaze.

Stefano took her hand. Without a word, he led her past the crowd, off the dance floor. He drew Tess past the tables and guests. Her full white satin skirts shimmered beneath the lights of the glittering crystal chandeliers as he pulled her away from the gilded ballroom and out a side door, into a shadowy back service hallway.

Once they were alone, his restraint fled.

He pushed her roughly against the wall, kissing her hard, gripping her wrists. She kissed him back with fury, surrendering to the angry force of her own desire.

"You're mine," he growled, kissing down her throat. "Say it, Tess."

Her head fell back as her veil tumbled and twisted around them.

"Yours," she breathed, and knew she was lost.

CHAPTER FIVE

As STEFANO KISSED down her throat, stroking the silky fabric of her dress, Tess closed her eyes, her body taut with need. She gasped as she felt the rough heat of his hands beneath the sweetheart neckline of her bodice, against her naked breasts.

Through the closed side door, she could hear the muffled sounds of music, laughter, dancing from the distant ballroom. The sounds of their wedding reception, still carrying on without them.

Here in this quiet, darkened hallway, they were alone. He swayed against her, and even through her thick white skirts, she could feel the force of his desire for her. They gripped each other, panting in the intensity of their need.

Abruptly he lifted her up against the wall. Her white skirts parted, her legs wrapped around his hips of their own accord. She felt his shaft pressing hard against her, through his trousers and the flimsy fabric of her panties.

Lowering his head, he kissed her passionately. Her fingertips dug into the shoulders of his tuxedo jacket. She wanted him closer, wanted *more*. With a low growl, he unzipped his fly.

Holding her backside, he pressed her hard against the wall. He shoved her delicate lace panties aside and pushed his enormous shaft inside her, filling her slowly, inch by delicious inch.

She gasped as she felt him hard and thick inside her, stretching her to the limit. Drawing back, he thrust again, even more deeply inside her wet, aching core. Desperate need pounded through her. She choked out a cry, gripping his shoulders.

His thrusts became harder, faster, as her white satin skirts shook and fluttered around them, the fabric opalescent and gleaming in the pale shadows of the hallway. Her breaths came in ragged gasps, her full breasts overflowing the low-cut neckline of the boned corset, a sliver of her pink nipples now visible.

Feeling him so deep inside her, all the way to her heart, pleasure blazed through her like a wildfire, consuming her. She'd wanted him for so long.

The wickedness of letting him do this to her when she hated him, when any moment someone might come into the hallway and see them, should have made her pull back and push him away. Instead, she only wanted him more.

Three more deep thrusts and she exploded in a shuddering cry, digging her nails into the expensive fabric of his tuxedo jacket. At that, he shoved himself inside her with a harsh shout, gripping her against the wall, his eyes closed with fierce ecstasy.

Tess slowly came back to earth, literally, as he released his grip on her thighs, letting her feet slide back to the floor.

His large hands smoothed her frothy white skirts neatly back down, as if nothing had happened. Turning away, he zipped up his tuxedo trousers. Watching him, Tess leaned back heavily against the wall, hardly able to believe what had just happened.

"I was never going to let you touch me again," she whispered.

Stefano glanced at her out of the corner of his eye. His cruel, sensual lips lifted into a cold smile. "If this is you hating me, I like it so far."

With a humiliated gasp, Tess turned away. He grabbed her wrist.

"Wait." His voice was low, and his earlier expression was gone, replaced with some emotion she couldn't identify. "Don't go. I didn't mean it."

"You did that just to show your control over me," she choked out, wiping her eyes, knowing she was probably streaking mascara across her face.

"Is that what you think?"

"What else could it be?"

He snorted, shaking his head. "I didn't even show control over *myself.* I meant to take you upstairs to the suite." He gave a rueful laugh. "I didn't quite make it."

Tess's cheeks were hot as she looked down

at the patterns of the carpet. "You blackmailed me into marriage," she said in a low voice. "You threatened to destroy my family, to take Esme away."

"It was an empty threat." He looked at her with glittering eyes. "I would never take Esme away from you, Tess. Not for any reason."

Shocked at this admission, Tess demanded, "Then why did you say it?"

"You were threatening to call off our wedding."

"We barely know each other. All I did was share some doubts. And you proved my fears right!"

"I don't want you to be afraid of me," he said quietly. "But I couldn't let you leave. Or Esme. I can't just abandon you to the whims of fate and hope you'll be safe. Marrying you is the only way I know to keep you safe." He gave her a regretful smile. "I'm sorry if my method was a bit unorthodox—"

"Unorthodox?"

"I'll make it up to you," he said in a low voice. "We have a lifetime. I know I can make you happy."

A lump rose in her throat at the certainty in his voice. "How can you be so sure?"

"You said you spent the last year thinking of me." Lifting his hand gently to her cheek, he said softly, "What you don't know is that I spent the last year trying not to think of you. And failing."

"What are you saying?"

"I never forgot you, Tess." He paused. "There's been no one else."

Was he saying…?

"Impossible," she breathed. "The model I saw you with yesterday—"

"Kebe?" He snorted. "She's just a kid. I was giving her a ride home from a party. Although," he murmured, grinning, "I like that you were jealous."

"I wasn't," she lied.

"Didn't my marriage proposal prove you're the only woman I'm interested in?"

"You proposed because of Esme."

"She's not the only reason." His hand stroked from the edge of her jawline to her sensitive lower lip. "You asked yesterday if I could be faithful to you. The truth is…" His dark gaze lifted to hers. "I have been. For over a year."

There was a noisy burst of conversation from the other end of the service hall as a group of uniformed waiters appeared, carrying trays. But Tess couldn't look away from his gaze. She was in shock.

Stefano took her hand with his own. "Come with me."

"We should go back to the reception," she said, trying to ignore the thrum of her heart. "People will be wondering where we are—"

"So?"

"Aren't they your friends?" she said, bewildered.

"Acquaintances. I don't give a damn about them. You're the only one I want to please."

"And Esme—"

"She's fine with your cousin, isn't she?"

"But…" She bit her lip. "What will my family think? Leaving my own wedding reception without a farewell?"

"It's your day, Tess. Your choice." His dark eyes seared her. "Do you want to go back and make small talk? Forget about what you think you're *supposed* to want. What do you *actually* want?"

Tess's lips parted. For so long, she'd worried about pleasing others. Always being cheerful, pleasant and helpful, no matter what. Maybe part of her had always been afraid that if she put one toe out of line her uncle and aunt might abandon her, as her father had, and send her away.

Raw emotion filled her. What did she want?

No one had ever really asked that before.

"I want to leave with you," she whispered. His dark eyes gleamed.

"Then come." His large hand enfolded her smaller one. As he pulled her down the shadowy hall, past the chattering waitstaff, it occurred to Tess that if their passionate interlude had taken any longer they would have put on a shockingly good show for a bunch of strangers. She should have felt ashamed.

But she wasn't. After a lifetime of feeling invisible and desperate to please, something had made her reckless and bold.

Not *something*.

Someone.

Stefano wasn't afraid of her expressing her true feelings, either good or bad. He was strong enough to take it. He didn't judge her. He wasn't going to punish her. He wasn't going to leave her.

You asked yesterday if I could be faithful to you. The truth is I have been. For over a year.

His husky words echoed through her as Stefano led her into the Campania's lobby. She shivered, hardly able to believe it was true. Stefano had been faithful to her for over a year?

Her hand tensed in his as he led her toward the elevator. Wealthy guests and elegant patrons at the lobby bar turned to gape openly at them, the famous billionaire prince and his redheaded bride in a diamond tiara and wedding gown. People started to whisper, to lift their phones to take pictures.

"Hurry," Stefano said in a low voice, picking up the pace. She raced with him, clinging to his hand, her white veil and white wedding skirts flying behind her.

As the elevator door closed behind them, he pulled her hungrily into his arms. He kissed her forehead, her temples, her eyelids. He cradled her in his arms as if she were a treasure and he never wanted to let her go. And then he kissed her lips.

As the elevator traveled upward, Tess felt her body surrender in his powerful arms. When he kissed her, she was lost.

How she wished she could still believe in her romantic fantasy of him, that he was a handsome prince on a white horse, a strong, romantic hero she could trust. How she wished she could just let herself go, let herself love that man…

But she couldn't. As he drew away from the kiss, Tess looked up at him. She couldn't even *think* about loving him. Not unless she wanted her heart to be broken again.

Because however she might feel in his arms, Stefano was no knight in shining armor. Just hours before, he'd blackmailed her into speaking their vows at their wedding ceremony. What should have been the happiest moment of Tess's life had instead been misery, an agony of hate and despair.

She couldn't let herself truly trust him. She couldn't let herself believe in the romance or give him her heart.

But as Stefano smiled down at her, his dark eyes gleaming wickedly, she felt breathless. Her heart pounded with emotion and desire.

She hated that he'd blackmailed her into marriage. But at least he'd done it for the right reason, she told herself. He wanted to protect her and

Esme, and claimed that he would spend the rest of his life making them happy. Could Tess truly fault him for that?

Especially when he made her feel like this...

As the elevator reached their floor, the door opened with a ding. Still holding her hand, Stefano led her toward his suite. After unlocking the door, he pushed it open. When Tess started to walk inside, he stopped her with a chiding smile. "That's not how it's done."

He picked her up in his arms as if she weighed nothing. Her long white veil and white skirts trailed behind them as he carried her over the threshold.

Inside, the suite, already so luxurious, had been utterly transformed. She gasped when she saw the lavish vases of long-stemmed red roses and soft glow of white candles.

"What have you done?" she breathed, looking up at him.

His eyes were dark, caressing her face. "For you," he said in a low voice. "All for you."

As the door closed behind them, he carried her past the main room, with its glittering view of the New York skyline at twilight, toward the bedroom.

Breathing in the scent of roses, Tess looked up at him as he carried her to bed. The flickering candles moved shadows across the chiseled planes of Stefano's high cheekbones and jawline. Like a medieval knight, she thought dreamily.

The bedroom, too, was filled with candles and roses. He set her gently on her feet, and she stepped out of her expensive white high heels. Looking down at her hungrily, he gently pulled out the pins that attached the diamond tiara and veil to her hair. He set them on the nightstand. The diamonds gleamed in the candlelight, the translucent veil lingering like a ghost against the marble floor.

Never looking away from her, he slowly took off his tuxedo jacket. He removed his platinum cuff links, one by one, setting them beside the tiara. He kicked off his expensive shoes, dropping his black tie to the floor.

All the while, she stood shivering in front of him in her wedding dress, knowing what was about to happen. Wanting it to happen.

Coming forward, he reached his arms around her and slowly unzipped the back of her wedding dress, letting it fall softly to the floor. Her shivering intensified as she stepped out of the gown and stood before him in her wedding lingerie.

She wasn't cold. His gaze was a blast of heat against her skin.

He'd picked out her lingerie. She'd blushed when she'd first tried it on. The structured bodice of her wedding gown had hidden a strapless bra that barely covered half of her breasts. And, more shocking still, there were slits in the white silk so her pink nipples peeked through the fabric.

Her panties were nearly as bad, just a little sliver of silk, loosely attached to white garters that held her shimmering stockings to her thighs.

Feeling his gaze in the flickering candlelight, she started to take off her bra.

"No," he said hoarsely. "Leave it."

Reaching up, Stefano loosened her chignon so that her red hair tumbled down around her shoulders in a cloud of scarlet.

"So beautiful," he breathed. Lifting her gently in his arms, he set her down on the enormous bed.

"So are you," she said shyly.

"You're mine now. To do with as I please."

She lifted her chin, and repeated, "So are you."

With a jagged intake of breath, he ripped off his crisp white shirt so swiftly she heard buttons hit the floor. Climbing beside her on the bed, he pushed her back against the mattress, lowering his mouth hungrily to hers.

She braced herself, expecting his embrace to be savage, for him to demand, to ruthlessly *take*, as he had in the hallway outside the ballroom.

But this time was different.

He gave, rather than took; he tempted, rather than plundered. His hands were gentle, caressing every inch of her naked body, even and especially the secret places barely covered by the sliding whispers of silk.

He seduced her slowly. Unsnapping her garter belt, he pulled down her thigh-high stockings, one by one, teasing her until she was panting with need.

He didn't demand what was his by right. Instead, he begged her with his touch.

And all along, she could feel his desire for her, fiercely contained. How was it possible that he already wanted her again? But he did. He did not bother to hide it. He caressed her with agonizing slowness, taking his time, as if he intended to make their pleasures last forever.

They could, she realized. They were married. They had all the time in the world.

Reaching up, she kissed him, caressing his sharp jawline, rough with five-o'clock shadow. She ran her hands down his back, over his warm skin, feeling the hard power of the muscles of his shoulders and biceps.

With a low growl, he rolled her over so she was above him on the bed. A moment before, trapped beneath his weight, she'd felt bold, unrestrained. Now, as she sat astride him, she stroked her fingertips tentatively down his bare chest, then stopped, biting her lip.

"What do you want me to do?" she whispered.

His dark eyes glinted up at her in the flickering candlelight. "Take what you want."

Reaching up to cup her full breasts through the bra, he lifted his head and gave one pebbled nipple a lick where it peeked through the slit in the silk, then moved to the other. She closed her eyes at the hot sizzle of pleasure spiraling in waves down her body.

Hesitantly she ran her hand down his powerful chest, lightly dusted with dark hair, to his flat, muscular belly. With her legs straddled over his hips, she could feel the hard thickness of his desire, feel the involuntary movement of him between her thighs.

Lowering her head with a tumble of her red hair against the pillow, she kissed his mouth, daringly teasing him with her tongue. He responded hungrily, kissing her long and hard. Reaching around her, he roughly unhooked the peek-a-boo bra and tossed the flimsy fabric to the floor. She relished the feel of her full naked breasts crushed against him, her tight, aching nipples brushing his hard chest. Instinctively, her hips swayed.

A choked gasp came from the back of his throat. Innocent as she still was, she suddenly realized her power over him. And she gloried in it.

She reached down to unzip his fly. With deliberate slowness, turnabout being fair game, she slid his tuxedo trousers and silk boxers down his legs, inch by inch.

Tossing them to the floor, she looked down at him in the candlelit shadows of the bedroom. He was a completely naked, magnificent male, his shaft jutting huge and hard from his body. She moved forward, intending to taste him even there, to tease him with her lips and hands. But, here, his patience ended.

With a low growl, he ripped off her white silk panties in a violent gesture, leaving the expensive garment nothing but tatters and ripped threads. Reaching around her hips, he lifted her up from his body, then pushed her back down against him, entering her.

Slowly.

Deliciously.

She gasped with pleasure, closing her eyes with ecstasy as he filled her so deeply—deeper still—stretching her all the way to the hilt.

As tension coiled tightly inside her, he gripped her hips, guiding her to ride him. She panted with the agonizing sweetness of the sensation. He felt huge beneath her, inside her. Leaning forward, she kissed him, trying desperately to hold herself back, to control the rhythm. But the pleasure was too great. Her body tightened, going higher and higher with rapidly exploding desire, and spiraled out of her control.

"Tess," he breathed beneath her in the dark. Thrusting deeply, he groaned her name. *"Tess."*

Something broke in her heart, rising from her soul like the sun after a storm. Joy burst through her, and all the broken little pieces of her soul came together in a bright blinding light. They were married. The two of them together made one—

A cry came from the back of her throat, rising to a scream that she did not recognize as her own as she exploded. In the same instant, he roared in harmony to her cry.

With a harsh intake of breath, she collapsed over him, exhausted, spent. Her limbs felt boneless.

Slowly his powerful arms reached up to wrap around her tenderly. For a long time, he held her, both of them naked in the candlelit bedroom. She heard only his rough breath, felt only the power of his body, lifting her with the rise and fall of his chest.

The next evening, as the chauffeur drove them through the streets of London, Stefano saw the awe in Tess's eyes and felt a strange thrill of wonder. It was almost like he, too, was seeing the glittering sights of London for the first time. Big Ben, Tower Bridge, the Tower of London, Trafalgar Square, Buckingham Palace.

"I've never seen anything like it," she breathed.

"You're a New York girl," he teased. "Surely you're not so easily impressed."

"This city is thousands of years old," she informed him archly.

"What were you reading on the plane? The history of London?"

"I was reading a novel. Louisa told me." Louisa was the flight attendant on their private jet. "London was founded by the ancient Romans!"

"So really," he said lazily, "we should get credit."

"You?"

"Italians." He reached past the baby to put his hand tenderly on his wife's knee. "Just wait until London Fashion Week. Are you excited?"

"Yes." Looking at his hand, she blushed, biting her lip. "Very."

And well she should blush, Stefano thought smugly, after the night they'd had. It had been the most amazing twenty-four hours of his life, even better than their first time. He'd made love to her four times last night in the hotel, then twice in the private bedroom in the back of the jet as they crossed the Atlantic. *His wife.* He couldn't get enough of her.

He shivered, remembering.

"I can't wait to see everything," she said softly, looking out at the city. "London, Milan, Paris. I can't believe I'll be attending three different Fashion Weeks, back to back."

"You never attended the one in New York?"

She snorted. "Fashion Week is for famous people, not poor design students. I've seen pictures on social media, though. I always wondered what it would be like."

"To see a runway show?"

"To hold one of my own." She gave him a wistful smile. "To be a designer for a major house."

Was she hinting that she wanted a job at Mercurio or Fontana? No, surely not. Why would Tess want to work, to hold down a grueling job with long hours that often paid little, when she could live with him in luxury? Stefano smiled at her. "You'll meet Mercurio's new designer in Paris," he said huskily. "And see all the shows up close."

Tess returned his smile. "Do you usually sit in the front row?"

He shrugged. "I could. But I generally leave that to celebrities. I prefer to be in the second row. I don't need to be photographed. I'm there for business."

"And to check out your rivals?" she said, handing their cooing baby a giraffe toy.

He gave Tess a startled look. She grinned, then said cheerfully, "I used to buy pastries from the bakery down the block for that exact same reason."

How funny she was, Stefano thought, his gaze tracing her sweet, pretty face, her pink lips, swollen from a night of kisses. His body stirred again.

It amazed him that he could still want her, after the night they'd had. He'd married Tess out of sense of duty, and because he desired her. What he hadn't expected was that he'd enjoy her company so much, even in the daytime. Talking with her. Being with her.

Somehow, Tess made everything in Stefano's life, everything he'd previously been bored with, seem different and new.

Climbing aboard their private jet in New York that morning, Tess had exclaimed over its large, luxurious cabin, newly outfitted with a travel crib and baby toys. Her eyes had been wide as saucers.

"First time on a private jet?" he'd asked her, smiling.

"First time on a plane!"

It was no wonder she'd been excited. When the flight attendant had offered to make them drinks and dinner, Tess had followed Louisa into the galley, to "help." Stefano was mystified. He always kept a distance from his own employees, even if they'd worked for him for years. His executive assistant, Agathe Durand, had been with him for fifteen years, but until her grandson became seriously ill last year, Stefano had known almost nothing about her family. He respected his employees' right to privacy and expected them to respect his. Tess obviously felt differently. By the end of the flight, Tess and the flight attendant were apparently best friends.

The flight attendant glowed under Tess's friendly attention, and so did the two pilots, at her over-the-top praise. Tess's sweet, hopeful nature was like sunshine, he realized, making everyone happier around her. Opening people's hearts.

Not his, of course. He didn't have a heart, so he was immune. But he enjoyed the effect she had on others. He was amused by her company and enjoyed the novelty of looking at the world through her less cynical eyes. Her warmth and idealistic heart were good qualities for a wife and mother.

Plus, she blew his mind in bed.

Stefano glanced at her now, sitting on the other side of the baby's car seat in the back of the Bentley. She was exclaiming over everything—even ordinary things such as red post boxes and black taxi cabs. Feeling his gaze, she gave him a happy smile, but he saw faint shadows beneath her eyes. As much time as they'd spent in bed, they hadn't slept a great deal. He was used to taking business calls and discussing the latest numbers at all hours, but he'd been surprised to discover Tess was awake just as much with the baby. He was accustomed to pushing himself to the limit, but he wanted Tess to be comfortable. He'd already sent a message to his assistant to find a nanny as soon as possible.

"What's that?" As the car slowed, Tess craned her neck to look out their window.

He smiled. "Our hotel."

"Wow," she breathed, looking up at the grand Victorian hotel, its stone turrets towering over them.

After the Bentley stopped, the hotel's uniformed doorman opened the door. After unbuckling the baby seat, Tess let him help her out, with Esme in her arms.

"Welcome to the Leighton Hotel London, madam," the doorman said, then bowed to Stefano. "Welcome back, Your Highness."

"Hello, Walter. This is my wife."

The doorman's eyes widened and he corrected himself, bowing to her, too. "Your Highness, welcome."

"Nice to meet you, Walter," she said warmly, then took Stefano's arm as he led her into the Leighton's grand, gilded lobby. The service was impeccable, as always. They were whisked upstairs without even having to pause at the registration desk, with their luggage and new stroller brought behind them.

Stefano always stayed in the same penthouse suite in London. As they entered the door, he smiled at her, his eyes twinkling. "Will this do for a honeymoon?"

Holding their babbling baby against her hip,

Tess walked through the suite's five elegant rooms and terrace overlooking Hyde Park. "Wow," she breathed again. Then she saw the flower arrangements and fruit baskets on the suite's gleaming wooden table. "What are these?"

"Congratulations on our marriage, I imagine. From friends who couldn't attend the ceremony. And business acquaintances." Coming forward, he kissed her. "Welcome to London, *cara mia.*" He kissed Esme's fat cheek tenderly. "And you, *mia figlia.*"

"Bah," said the baby, waving her chunky arms at his nose.

There was a peremptory knock at the door of the suite, and a chic white-haired woman entered, followed by a plump middle-aged blonde.

"Tess," he said, and took his wife's hand, "I'd like you to meet my executive assistant, Agathe Durand."

"Congratulations again, Your Highness," said the white-haired woman.

"Thank you, Agathe." He looked next at the plump blonde. "This is the nanny?"

"Yes, sir."

"Nanny?" said Tess.

"I am most pleased to meet you, Your Highness," the executive assistant said to Tess with a nod, then motioned to the middle-aged woman behind her. "This is Ann Carter, from the most respected nanny service in London. She'll be traveling with your family for the next month."

"Lovely to meet you, Your Highness." The nanny's smile was kind. She looked at the baby. "And this is the little one?"

"Er…hello." Still holding Esme tight, Tess turned to Stefano with a bewildered frown. "Why do we need a nanny? Unless—" She brightened. "Are you offering me a job as a designer? Oh, Stefano!" Joy lit up her face. "You don't know what this means to me. I don't need any special treatment. I'll be happy to be assistant to an assistant—"

Stefano cut her off with a scowl. "You don't need to work, Tess. I can more than provide for you."

Her face fell. "Then why a nanny?"

He could hardly explain that he wanted to give her more time for sex and sleep, not with his employees listening to every word. So he stuck to half the truth. "As my wife, you'll often have PR events to attend. Runway shows. Parties. Charity balls." He grinned. "Art Basel. Weekends on the French Riviera or yachting on the Costa Smeralda."

"Me?" Tess looked flabbergasted. "I'll be doing those things?"

"You're joining my life, and that's how I live. Starting with a party tonight. You remember the woman who attended our wedding, Fenella Montfort?"

Tess's face was blank. "Um. Maybe?"

"It's fine. You were distracted." He smiled. "She's the primary shareholder of Zacco. Our lawyers have already started negotiations, but the company is hosting a party at her town house tonight, and I hoped…"

"You hoped to use your charm to jump-start the negotiations?"

"Exactly."

Tess looked at him and sighed. "Then of course we must go."

Taking her hand in his own, he kissed it. "Thank you, *cara*. I knew you would understand."

"Don't worry, Your Highness," Ann Carter said, holding out her arms for Esme.

With some visible reluctance, Tess handed her the baby as the nanny continued talking.

"I've been caring for babies my whole life." She smiled down at Esme. "We'll get along very well, won't we? Shall we go read stories in the nursery?"

The baby gurgled with delight, waving her pudgy arms.

Tess watched them, biting her lip. Stefano could see she was nervous at the thought of leaving their daughter with anyone besides family or friends.

"It'll be all right," Stefano said, touching her

shoulder. "The party isn't far. We don't have to be out late."

She took a deep breath. "All right." She gave him a wan smile. "This party is important, right?"

"It is." Drawing her close, he kissed her on the forehead. "Thank you."

Thirty minutes later, he and Tess left the hotel in a luxury limousine. The burly bodyguard he kept on staff in Europe, Leon Rossi, sat in front beside the driver.

Leaning close to Stefano in the back seat, Tess whispered, "Why a bodyguard?"

"Don't worry." Stefano looked down at her. "He'll wait in the car. There's no threat. It's simply best practice."

"You mean, all the other billionaires had a bodyguard, so you wanted one, too."

"Well…yes." A smile lifted the corners of his lips. "And I wanted the best. I stole Leon away from his previous employer. Who was that again, Leon?"

"Cristiano Moretti, boss."

Folding her arms, Tess shook her head, her eyes gleaming with amusement. "You're incorrigible."

"See? You do know me."

Stefano couldn't stop looking at her. Tess was wearing a new dress, chosen from a selection sent up by the hotel's luxury boutique. He'd offered to arrange a stylist, but Tess had refused. She'd done her own hair and makeup in twenty minutes. And she was the most impossibly beautiful woman he'd ever seen.

Her bright red hair tumbled down her shoulders, and her ruby lips were full and ripe. Her bright green eyes stood out like emeralds, lined with black against her fair skin. Her hourglass figure was lush and enticing in the strapless sapphire-blue dress. A faux fur stole was draped around her bare shoulders to keep out the cool, slightly drizzly air of an autumn night in London.

Stefano felt intoxicated with pride. Lowering his head, he kissed her, relishing the sweet taste of her soft lips.

He drew back with a sigh. "I almost wish we didn't have to go tonight."

"This Montfort woman, what's she like?"

He smiled down at her, running his hands through her silky hair. "Even more ruthless than her father. He was the one who bought Zacco. She took over after he retired."

"Is she married?"

"Why?" His smile broadened. "Are you jealous?"

"Just wondering," she said evasively. The lights of the city passed over her lovely face as the limo drove through the London night.

"As far as I can tell, she's a workaholic. It's a

pity." He sighed. "Zacco has done exceptionally well with her as CEO."

"Why is that a pity?"

"Business is booming, which is reflected in Zacco's stock price, and will make it harder to convince her to sell. But I assure you," he whispered, cradling her cheek, "you have nothing to worry about, *cara*. All I want from her is Zacco. Believe me."

She bit her plump, pink lower lip. "And what do you want from me?"

"From you?" he said huskily. "Everything."

He kissed her again, deeply. It was far easier to take her in his arms with no baby seat between them in the back seat. When the limo stopped, it took him a moment to notice. The back door opened, but he didn't feel the cold air.

The driver politely cleared his throat. "We're here, Your Highness."

Reluctantly Stefano pulled away from the embrace and tenderly rubbed away a smear of lipstick from Tess's cheek. At the same moment she reached up and wiped it off his lips. Looking at each other, they gave an awkward laugh. Then, after getting out of the car, he held out his arm. "Come," he said in a low voice. "I can hardly wait to introduce you."

CHAPTER SIX

STEFANO THOUGHT HE knew luxury, but this was truly over the top.

The Zacco party was in full swing at Fenella Montfort's luxurious, five-story town house near Kensington Palace. Everything was lavish, from the flowers to the champagne to the army of uniformed servants. He himself certainly had his share of household employees, but Fenella's party was staffed at levels that made *Downton Abbey* look chintzy.

Everywhere he looked, he saw the Zacco brand. Everything from pillows to brocade curtains was festooned with the famous curlicue Zs.

Stefano's stomach clenched. He thought of how his lawyers' negotiations had already stalled. Fenella's lawyers were stonewalling, claiming she had no desire to sell. Zacco, always glamorous, had become wildly fashionable since Fenella had become CEO.

The offbeat, colorful, ridiculously expensive clothes were now splashed all over magazine covers, trendy with Hollywood, old-money and social-media celebrities alike. The stock price had increased 20 percent in the last year.

In that same time, Stefano's own new fashion brand, Mercurio, had tanked. Their previous creative director's lackluster designs had done poorly in every market. It took a special sort of skill, he thought grimly, to bomb simultaneously on every continent at once.

He consoled himself with the thought that Mercurio's new collection, to be debuted in two weeks in Paris by the hot young designer he'd recently hired, would soon get the company back on track.

But the truth was Mercurio meant nothing to him compared to the brand that bore his family name. He had to get Zacco back at any price. If he couldn't, what had he been working for all these years? What was the point of success if he couldn't get what he wanted most?

"Your Highness!" a well-known German artist greeted him, shaking hands.

"Stefano—good to see you!" A famous model kissed him on each cheek, then, before Tess could decide to be jealous, the model kissed her exactly the same way and moved on to the next person.

A glamorous older woman with hip-length black hair walked by, trailing an entourage of wildly dressed young people. The woman paused when she saw Stefano.

"Your Highness," she said, nodding her head briefly.

"Mrs. Sakurai," he said, with the same respectful nod.

The woman glanced at Tess without recognition, then continued through the party with her entourage and a crowd of adoring fans in her wake.

Stefano turned to Tess. "That woman is—"

"Aiko Sakurai," she breathed, staring after her. Stefano's eyes widened.

"You know her?"

"I studied her in design school. She's amazing. Her designs—" Tess shook her head. "I could only wish to be half so talented as her."

"She's older than you," he pointed out. "She's had more experience."

"What she's done as Zacco's creative director isn't just experience. It's genius."

"Yes, unfortunately. Thanks to her, Zacco's valuation has gone up billions and become completely unaffordable," he said grumpily. Catching himself, he looked down at Tess with a smile. "Come. There are others I want you to meet."

For the next hour, they drank cocktails as he introduced her to CEOs and friends and journalists, all members of the international fashion jet set. They congratulated them on their marriage and were eager to meet Tess. No wonder, he thought. With his wife's warmth and beauty and charm, not to mention the inherent star power of being the unknown working-class Brooklyn girl who'd managed to tame a playboy like Stefano, Tess was quickly the most popular person in the room.

Stefano watched Tess affectionately as she spoke earnestly to a famous South African designer. She wasn't intimidated by anyone. She treated everyone the same, from billionaires to waitstaff. Stefano liked that about her. Her honesty, her kindness. Even at a party filled with some of the most gorgeous, glamorous people in the world, he thought, no one could hold a candle to his wife.

But where was their hostess? He scoured the crowd for Fenella Montfort's tall, spare frame. He finally saw the woman talking to a prime minister and Rodrigo Cabrera, the Spanish media mogul.

Setting his jaw, Stefano went to join them.

"Good evening." He nodded at each. "Your Excellency... Cabrera." His eyes focused on his quarry. "Ms. Montfort."

"I hear you're married, Prince Stefano," Rodrigo Cabrera said, his eyes glinting. "Congratulations."

"Thank you." He lifted his eyebrows. "Actually, you should doubly be thanked, Cabrera, since I met my wife at your party."

The Spaniard looked intrigued. "My party?"

"Last summer, in New York. You were celebrating some movie of yours that had just reached a billion dollars box office worldwide. Tess was a waitress there."

"How extraordinary."

"Yes." But as Stefano spoke, he was wondering how he could speak with Fenella Montfort alone, though Zacco's London Fashion Week party did seem an inappropriate venue to convince her to sell her shares.

She gave him a cold smile, as if she knew exactly what he was thinking.

"Excuse us," she said abruptly to the other two men. "Prince Stefano and I have something important to discuss."

"Of course," said the prime minister with a bow.

"Congratulations again," Rodrigo Cabrera said coolly. "Actually making it to the altar is quite an accomplishment."

It seemed a strange comment, but Stefano forgot about it as he faced the woman who owned his family's company.

"Prince Stefano," she said coolly. "I'm so glad you brought your new wife. Such a fascinating creature." She glanced toward Tess. "A true original."

"Thank you."

"It wasn't a compliment." She jutted her sharp

chin toward a young, dark-haired man flirting with models by the marble fireplace. "That's my date. Bruno."

"Ah," he replied, unsure of her point. Why would he care about her date?

Fenella gave a laugh. "He's a musician. But a good lover." She paused. "I can't imagine being stupid enough to marry him."

Stefano's shoulders tightened as he understood. She was insulting not just Tess, but also him, for marrying her.

What he didn't understand was why. He barely knew Fenella Montfort. They were business acquaintances only. What could be the point of an attack that was so personal and so pointless?

He tried to keep his voice conciliatory. "As fascinating as it is to discuss our love lives, we need to talk about your shares."

"Yes, we do." She tilted her head. "Please tell your lawyers to stop bothering us. It's tiresome."

"We can raise the offer."

"I don't intend to sell. At any price."

"You haven't heard the new offer," he said.

She shrugged. "I don't need to."

He narrowed his eyes. "Then why did you invite me tonight?"

"I wanted to tell you in person."

"No. There's something else."

Fenella's eyes gleamed. "You're right, of course."

She tilted her head. "I'm throwing the fashion journalists a bone. Having you at the party gives them drama to write about. The handsome billionaire prince attending a party for the company his family lost. Your presence makes the Zacco brand seem even more valuable. That's what really matters, isn't it?" Watching him, she smiled. "The success of my brand."

Her brand.

She'd lured him here as an insult, he realized. A taunt.

A rush of anger went through Stefano's heart. He controlled it, giving her a ruthless smile. "In that case, I wish you good evening, Ms. Montfort."

She sipped her champagne. "And you, Your Highness."

Turning away stiffly, he set down his own half-empty glass and strode through the crowd of people until he found his wife. He took Tess by the elbow. "Let's go."

"Go?" She'd been having a good time talking to all the people around her. She looked disappointed. "Right now?"

"Right now," he said grimly.

As the limo returned them to Mayfair, Stefano stared out at the sparkling London night.

The handsome billionaire prince attending a party for the company his family lost. Your presence makes the Zacco brand seem even more valuable. That's what really matters, isn't it? The success of my brand.

The memory of Fenella's taunting voice echoed through him as they drove through the city. Tess, after a few attempts to talk to him, finally gave up. The evening, which had begun in such hopeful pleasure, ended in silence.

Once they arrived back at their hotel suite, Tess rushed to check on their sleeping baby. Ann Carter rose to her feet from the chair where she'd been knitting some baby-sized slippers. Esme had obviously been well cared for.

Stefano spoke to her quietly, then the woman left for her own hotel suite on another floor. It would cost an exorbitant amount to have her on retainer for the next month, but, to Stefano, no price was too high for his child's or his wife's comfort. He'd always believed the cliché: *You get what you pay for.*

But he'd never imagined Fenella Montfort would refuse to sell at any price. How could she?

Pulling off his black tie, he walked heavily to the bedroom. He tossed down his jacket. His jaw was hard as he looked at himself in the shadowy mirror.

He had to find a way. He *would*. By right, Zacco belonged to him. It was his family's company, their legacy.

He had expected Tess to join him in the bedroom. When she did not, he went looking for her. The nursery was dark, the only sound Esme's gentle snores. The main room was empty.

He finally found Tess on the moonlit terrace overlooking Hyde Park. She was hugging the faux fur stole around her shoulders, looking out into the night.

"What are you doing out here?"

Squaring her shoulders, she faced him quietly. "What happened tonight?"

"What do you mean?"

"Why did we leave so suddenly?"

Stefano was tempted to deny, to bluster, to evade. To stonewall.

Instead, he heard himself say, "Fenella Montfort won't sell Zacco."

Tess's eyes widened. He waited for her to say something flippant. Instead, coming forward, wordlessly she wrapped her arms around him.

For a moment, he closed his eyes, accepting the offered comfort. Then he drew back, tightening his jaw. "I'll find a way to convince her."

"And if you don't?"

"I will."

"You already have so much," Tess said slowly. "Mercurio, Fontana. Real estate, companies that sell sports cars, jewelry. Do you really need Zacco back that badly?" Searching his gaze, she said, "Couldn't you just let it go?"

"No," he said.

"Why?"

He looked out briefly toward the darkness of Hyde Park.

"My father ignored everything except his pleasures—mistresses, love affairs. He left me to be raised by servants and sold off the family business to finance his sybaritic lifestyle." His hands clenched. "I want it back."

"I get it," Tess said suddenly. "You want to make it right. To get back what you lost."

Stefano looked at her sharply. She gave him a sympathetic smile.

"I never knew my father," she said. "My mother raised me alone. When I was twelve, she died." She looked down, her arms crossed over her chest, gripping the ends of the stole around her shoulders. "After her funeral, I thought my father would finally come for me. But he…he didn't. I found out later he was already married, with another family."

Stefano hated the pain in her eyes. "He was wrong. Both to you, and to his wife. He acted without honor."

"He was still my father." She gave a wistful, bitter smile. "After my mother's funeral, I tried to barricade myself in our apartment with books, so that my uncle wouldn't take me to Brooklyn. Because I was so sure my father would come. But he didn't want me to exist, so he pretended I didn't."

Moonlight illuminated her beautiful face, showing a single tear streaking down her cheek as they stood together on the dark, quiet terrace.

"He was a fool," he said quietly.

Tess took a deep breath. "The point is, sometimes you can't get back the things you've lost. No matter how hard you try. All you can do is try to move on, move forward." She looked out toward the moonlit park. "If my aunt and uncle hadn't taken me in, I don't know what would have happened to me. Although…"

"Although?"

She gave him a wistful smile. "Sometimes it was hard to always feel so indebted to them. To be afraid that if I made one false step they might send me away."

A silent curse went through him. No wonder she'd fallen in love so easily the night he'd seduced her. She'd been hungry for a place—a person— to call her own. Someone with her by choice, not duty. Taking her into his arms, he said quietly, "I'm sorry."

"Don't be." She lifted her gaze to his. "It's all worked out, hasn't it? We're married now. Raising Esme together." She interlaced his hands with her own. "We'll give her a better childhood than we had. She'll always know she's loved—by both of us."

"Yes," Stefano said. The word *love* made him

uncomfortable. He cared for Esme, yes, and he felt his responsibility acutely to provide for her and protect her as a father. Was that the same as love?

"We're each other's family now," Tess said, her eyes shining, and his heart tightened even more. "All the pain is in the past. The future is filled with love—"

"Look, Tess," he interrupted. "You know I'm not good with…" He couldn't say the word *love*. "With feelings, right? Emotions?"

She looked at him, uncomprehending.

"I just don't want you to get the wrong idea," he said. "Like you did our first night, when you suddenly claimed you loved me. I wanted to see you again. But after that, I couldn't."

All the color drained from Tess's face.

"That's why you never called me again?" she whispered. "Because I said I was falling in love with you?"

He shrugged. "Look, I know that's all in the past. We're married now. We have a life together, a child. So I want to make sure we understand each other. I like you a lot, Tess." He gave her a wicked grin. "Especially in bed. But that's all I'm capable of. Passion. Partnership. Parenthood."

Her pale cheeks flushed red. She gave a strange laugh, pulling away. "I know that. Do you seriously think I don't know that? I'd never be tempted to love you again. Not now I know you!"

"Good," he agreed, relieved. "I just wanted to be sure. I'd never want to make you unhappy or break your heart."

"You, break my heart? Not likely!" Turning away, Tess changed the subject. "So what will you do about Zacco?"

"Convince her to sell," Stefano said.

"How?"

"The same way I do everything." He spoke lightly, but his smile was grim. "At any price."

Tess had gambled, marrying him. She'd gambled and lost.

Her husband would never love her. He couldn't love her. When she'd naively blurted out that she was falling in love with him, after their first night together, he'd ruthlessly cut her out of his life.

Just that had made him disappear.

I like you a lot, Tess. Especially in bed. But that's all I'm capable of. Passion. Partnership. Parenthood.

For Tess's whole life, she'd dreamed of loving someone and being loved in return. But, now, she would never know what either felt like.

Because if her husband couldn't love her, then she couldn't love him.

They would be friends. Partners. Spouses. Lovers. That was all.

But it was hard.

During their week in London, Tess spent every moment at Stefano's side, both by day, as he took her to runway shows, and by night, as they attended parties, then afterward, in bed, when he set her world on fire.

She saw his kindness when he thought no one was looking. To the outside world, Stefano tried to always look ruthless and tough. And he was, she knew. But there was also another side to him. He secretly helped people, without any benefit to himself.

His executive assistant, Agathe, had told Tess privately that when her young grandson had fallen desperately ill the previous year, Stefano had flown the boy to Switzerland and paid for him to get experimental treatment. Tears rose to the Frenchwoman's eyes. "My grandson might not be alive now if not for Prince Stefano's kindness. But he won't let me thank him, or even mention it."

It was a story Tess would hear again and again. The very next day, the head of a children's charity had come up to Tess at a party. "Prince Stefano has given our charity millions, but he insists on complete anonymity. He won't let us thank him, so I'm thanking you. He's made such a difference." Wiping his eyes, the elderly man had smiled. "But you're his wife. You know how he is."

She hadn't, though she was quickly learning.

Returning to the Leighton from a party, Stefano and Tess had overheard the night manager talking anxiously on the phone. He had a relative trapped in another country, and war had broken out. Stefano had interrupted. "Call this number," he'd said, handing the distraught manager a card. "Your relative will be evacuated within the day."

When the older man tried to tearfully thank him, Stefano brushed him off. "It's nothing. Anyone would do the same."

Tess doubted that. After all, the manager wasn't Stefano's friend or even his employee. He was simply someone who happened to work at Stefano's favorite London hotel. But Stefano chose to get involved.

At his own company, Gioreale S.p.A., she learned Stefano was revered for the way he promoted his employees, based not on who they knew or where they'd gone to school, but purely on their hard work and talent. The company's social marketing manager, a former addict who'd gone to prison for two years before getting clean, had made a point of finding Tess at a runway show to tell her, "No one else wanted to hire me, but Prince Stefano gave me a chance. He changed my life."

Over and over, she heard these whispered stories of secret kindness, of changed lives. But whenever she tried to ask Stefano about it, he was brusque.

"Don't be ridiculous. I hired Thomas Martin because he's the best damn social media director in Europe." He gave a swift smile. "You know me. I just want the best."

For some reason, he seemed embarrassed by his kindness, as if it was a weakness. But his employees worked hard to please him, and he returned their loyalty in full, paying them double what other firms paid. It was almost shocking, Tess thought, in this modern age, to see a boss who cared more about his employees than about maximizing every penny of profit.

Who wouldn't love a man like that?

Not her, Tess told herself stonily. She felt nothing for him at all, except—except friendship. And pride, perhaps, but who could blame her?

Their last morning in London, Tess woke up before dawn in their hotel suite, thinking she'd heard a noise from Esme's room. She yawned, glancing at the clock. It was just past four.

Stefano's side of the bed was empty. He'd made love to Tess before midnight, then she'd fallen asleep in his arms. He must have gotten up to make an overseas phone call, she thought, perhaps to the Tokyo office. His appetite for work was superhuman. It was what had made him so successful, but sometimes she wondered how anyone could work so hard, and sleep so little.

Blearily she stuck her feet into slippers and

pulled on a robe, then headed to Esme's room to feed and change her. She stopped when she heard a noise inside.

Peeking through the open door, she saw to her surprise that Stefano was sitting in the rocking chair, tenderly crooning an Italian lullaby to Esme. The baby, cradled against his powerful chest, was holding a bottle and staring up at her father with big, adoring eyes.

At the tender image, Tess's knees went weak. She closed her eyes, leaning against the hallway wall for support. Seeing the way he was caring for their child in the middle of the night, deliberately leaving Tess to sleep, made her eyes fill with tears.

Perhaps he didn't know how to love Tess. But he cared for her, and he loved their child.

Holding her breath, she watched as he rocked the baby to sleep, then took the empty bottle from her lips and lifted her carefully into the crib. For a moment, he watched their baby sleep, and Tess's heart swelled in her chest. Then, with a sigh, he started to turn.

Hurriedly Tess ducked back down the hall. Rushing back to their bedroom, she leaped into bed, pretending to be asleep in the dark. A moment later, she felt him climb into bed beside her.

"Stefano?" she whispered.

He paused. "I was just checking on the baby.

She's fine." He kissed her forehead. "Go back to sleep."

Who wouldn't love a man like that?

Not her, Tess repeated to herself desperately. She'd been burned. She'd been warned outright. She wasn't stupid enough to go back for second helpings of pain!

She liked him, that was all. They shared a child. Shared a life. She liked how he listened when she talked, as if every word she said was fascinating. She liked how he looked at her, as if she was the most beautiful creature in the world. She liked how he cared for their baby so carefully, learning how to be a father when he'd barely had one himself.

She wouldn't love him. Of course she would not.

Fiercely determined, she held back her heart. She felt like she was clinging to the edge of an abyss, with white knuckles. It almost seemed like he was taunting her, the way he'd suddenly become the man she'd always dreamed of. Desperately she looked for his flaws.

After London, they spent an idyllic week in Milan, attending the most important runway shows and parties, staying in the best suite in the best hotel in the city. See? Flaw!

"You always want the best of everything," Tess grumbled, rolling her eyes.

"Yes, I do," he said huskily, pulling her into his arms. "Why do you think I married you?"

He kissed her, his lips hot and smooth as silk. Another flaw, she thought. His kisses. They tempted her to believe lies and to want things she could not have. Specifically: his heart.

It was like he wanted to destroy her.

She hid her growing misery over the next week in Milan as she wore new couture dresses every night, made by famous Italian designers that she'd previously only seen in magazines. Stylists did her makeup and hair. With their wonderful nanny watching their contented baby, Tess and Stefano went out every night. She met fascinating people, made lots of new friends, ate delicious food and, best of all, wore designer clothes to every event. Clothes that felt like art.

Clothes that, in her growing panic, suddenly felt like her only escape.

Growing up, Tess had often played dress-up, trying on her mother's old costumes from an ancient trunk that had always come with them wherever they traveled.

After her mother died, her uncle had refused to allow Tess to bring the trunk into the already crowded apartment above the bakery. But Tess had never forgotten the difference clothes could make.

On the nights her mother performed on stage,

Tess had seen the transformation. Clothes could change who you were and who people took you to be. Clothes could make you appear—even make you *feel*—old or young, hopeful or sad, rich or poor. Clothes could make you stand out or they could make you disappear. During her lonely years in high school in Brooklyn, when she couldn't afford to buy new clothes, Tess had learned to sew.

Getting into fashion design school had been the happiest day of her life. She'd won a scholarship with her good grades, but she'd still had to scrimp and save for two years, which made her older than most of the other students. It had broken her heart when she'd had to give it up.

Now, as Tess attended runway shows and actually met the people who designed the clothes, all her old dreams came flooding back. Even the most famous designers hadn't always been famous, she realized. Once they had been just like her, with nothing but a dream.

Each night, after they returned to their hotel suite, she'd peek into her old suitcase, at the hand-made designs she couldn't leave behind. Her eyes always fell on a beautiful, shimmery green gown she'd made right after she'd dropped out of design school. Facing single motherhood without a career, she'd been discouraged and afraid. So she'd made the fairy-tale dress to give herself hope for the future.

She'd never gotten a chance to wear it. Since marrying Stefano, she'd only worn designer clothes from luxury brands. But each night she lightly touched the green dress. Maybe, someday, she'd wear it. Maybe, someday, she'd even design again. Maybe, someday, she'd be brave.

But not today. She was too busy spending every moment with the husband she wasn't allowed to love and with her baby, who had never seemed happier.

She could survive, Tess told herself. She could live without love. Her baby's happiness was worth any sacrifice.

She still got lots of attention. Whenever she and Stefano went out, people spoke to her warmly.

"Welcome, Your Highness."

"It's so good to see you again, Your Highness."

"You do us honor, Your Highness."

After so many years of living in her uncle's attic, feeling invisible and unwanted, it felt like warm sunshine after a long, cold winter.

Between fashion events, Stefano took Tess and Esme to see the sights of Milan. He seemed to relish her gasps at every tourist attraction. As she went into raptures over the Duomo or the Teatro alla Scala, he always kissed her, which made her blush. Which made him kiss her more.

Family was what mattered. Her baby's happiness mattered. Tess's romantic dreams? Those were in the past, to be put away like childhood toys.

But, sometimes, she had to hide how much it hurt.

Stefano wasn't always happy, either. She knew he was brooding about the upcoming Mercurio show and the stalled negotiations for Zacco. Sometimes, she caught him glaring at nothing, his hands clenched. Once she overheard him yelling at his lawyers. Apparently, they'd hit a brick wall. The Montfort woman was still flatly refusing to sell.

The afternoon before they left Milan, Stefano announced they needed a getaway and took them to a villa on Lake Como owned by one of his friends. There, their family had a picnic on the terrace, beneath a rose-covered trellis.

As their baby played, Tess looked out at the autumn sunlight shining off the lake, matching the soft glow in Stefano's dark eyes. Sitting beside her at the stone table, he took her in his arms as the first cold wind blew down from the mountains across Lake Como.

How can you be so cruel? Tess thought wildly, looking up into the gleam of his dark eyes. How can he look at me like that unless he loves me?

I just don't want you to get the wrong idea... I'd never want to make you unhappy or break your heart.

Remembering his words, she felt a chill. Whatever she imagined in his eyes, she couldn't let herself believe it. He'd told her outright not to love him. So she wouldn't. Her heart ached. What else could she believe in?

She had to find a new dream. But what?

Then she suddenly knew.

CHAPTER SEVEN

HANDS IN POCKETS, Stefano paced back and forth across his sprawling Paris apartment. He stopped, turning to glare at Tess, who was sitting in a chair, getting her hair and makeup done.

"Where is it?" he demanded for the tenth time. She gave him a tranquil smile.

"It will be here. Any minute."

"What's taking so long?" he growled, clawing back his hair. "We're supposed to leave in ten minutes."

"We have time."

He exhaled, grateful for Tess's calm smile. He didn't know what he'd do without her. It was funny, he thought. He'd owned this Paris apartment for years, the entire top floor of an exclusive building in the 7th arrondissement, with balconies overlooking the Eiffel Tower and autumn-hued trees of the Champ de Mars. It had never felt like home to him. Now, having a family here, it did. Esme didn't just have her own bedroom, she had her own nursery suite. Ann Carter was already there, playing with the baby.

"I'm dying to see Mercurio's new spring collection," said Genevieve Vincent, the stylist doing Tess's hair, a friend of his. She smiled, tilting her head. "I'm sure you've already seen it, Stefano. What's your honest opinion? I promise not to mention it in my blog—much."

"Sorry, Genevieve. I can't discuss it," Stefano said. "But it's going to be amazing."

"Really? So you *have* seen it." Genevieve looked hopeful. "*Amazing*, eh? Can I take that as a quote?"

He hesitated. The truth was, Caspar von Schreck, his new designer, had refused to let Stefano see any of the designs in advance, saying it would interfere with his creative process. But the man had promised to send samples of the best dresses for Tess to wear to the big runway show tonight.

The last thing Stefano needed was for rumors like "CEO tepid about new collection" to sink Mercurio's new season before it even started. Praise seemed safe enough.

"It's wonderful," he said firmly. "The whole world will be impressed. And, yes, quote me."

There was a hard knock at the door. The three of them looked at one another.

"See, Stefano?" Tess said cheerfully. "You worried over nothing!"

He heard his bodyguard in the foyer, answering the door. A moment later, Leon rolled in a large garment rack. The clothing was hidden by a thick canvas printed with the Mercurio logo of big block Ms.

"Finally," Stefano said under his breath. Hurrying forward, he yanked off the cover.

His eyes went wide. Only three hangers, looking forlorn, hung from the enormous rack. He grabbed the first dress, hoping to be reassured that the new collection would be the success that Mercurio—and he—so desperately needed.

But he couldn't make sense of it. He looked at the first dress, then the next, then the last. All three dresses were an unattractive shade of beige, with ragged, asymmetrical hems and strangely placed cutouts on the hips and breasts that seemed to defy the bounds of decency.

Genevieve stood beside him, her eyes wide. "Those are from Mercurio?"

Stefano bared his teeth in a smile. "Very…innovative, aren't they?"

"Innovative?" Tess stood on the other side of him now, her lovely face incredulous. "Are you crazy?" She looked at the three dresses with increasing desperation. "They're hideous!"

She was speaking his greatest fear aloud.

"Just choose one." His voice was harsh. "And get dressed. I'll check on the baby. Then we must go."

Stefano went down the hall, trying to keep calm. Outside the nursery door, he paused, taking several deep breaths, his hands clenched at his sides.

His designer knew what he was doing. The man was widely in demand. Everyone had said Caspar von Schreck was the best.

Obviously, Stefano must not understand the latest trends. And Tess and Genevieve didn't, either.

At least he prayed it was so. Or he was about to be humiliated. And when his conglomerate's share price plummeted, he'd literally pay the price.

Pushing the thought away, he smiled and went into the nursery. His baby daughter's face lit up when she saw him.

"Bah-bah!" she said, reaching for him.

"Good evening, Your Highness," the nanny said. "We were just reading a book."

"I see that." Lifting Esme up in his arms, he hugged her, breathing in the sweet smell of the baby's dark hair. His heart swelled with some emotion he didn't recognize—pride? Yes. It had to be pride. "*Buonanotte*," he whispered to her, then returned the baby to Ann Carter's arms.

As the nanny went back to reading a book about a duck and a truck, Stefano hesitated in the hallway. To his surprise, he almost wished he could stay. He wished he and Tess could be the ones to cuddle with Esme, and read her the story about the duck. Let Ann Carter go to the Mercurio show.

But that was ridiculous. What was he thinking? Straightening the cuffs of his sleek black jacket, he checked his platinum cuff links and wondered which dress Tess had chosen to wear. Luckily his wife was so beautiful that she'd make even a washed-out, raggedy gown look good.

When he came out of the hallway into the main room, he saw Genevieve packing up. Tess was ready, wrapped in a long black cape. He frowned.

"So, which dress did you choose?"

A determined look came over her beautiful face. "It's a surprise."

"But you did find one."

"Yes, I did." Her gaze was evasive. "I need to say good-night to Esme."

A moment later, they left his luxury apartment. Their bodyguard held an umbrella overhead to keep out the cold October drizzle, soft as mist. As their limousine drove them across Paris, Tess held her long cape carefully over her gown. She wouldn't let Stefano see even an inch of it.

She obviously desired to reveal her dress dramatically on the red carpet, he thought. It might have amused him if the stakes hadn't been so high. After all, how much surprise was possible, really? One beige dress was very like another.

Stefano looked out at the sparkling City of Light, thinking how important tonight's event was, not just to Mercurio, but to him personally.

If Caspar von Schreck's new spring collection was a success, then Mercurio would flourish. Which meant the stock of Stefano's parent company, Gioreale S.p.A, would rise. He'd be able to use it as collateral to make a new, higher offer to acquire Zacco from Fenella Montfort.

But if tonight wasn't a success...

His hands tightened.

It just had to be.

Caspar von Schreck was the best, he repeated to himself. He was the hottest designer in the world. Everyone said so. How could it possibly fail?

The limo finally pulled up in front of the glamorous *palais* where the Mercurio show was being held. With all the secrecy and buzz, it had become the most-anticipated event of Paris Fashion Week.

The bodyguard opened his door. Buttoning his jacket, Stefano smoothed a confident smile over his features and stepped out.

The rain had stopped. Crowds cheered, recognizing him. So far, so good. Giving the crowd a short wave, he turned back to Tess. As he helped his wife out of the limo and onto the red carpet, cameras flashed and reporters shouted questions.

Ignoring them, Stefano looked down at his beautiful wife. He felt a flash of comfort. At least, no matter what, she was completely on his side.

Looking nervous but determined, Tess lifted her chin, then dropped the long black cape onto the red carpet.

Stefano's jaw dropped as he saw her dress.

Not beige.

Not ragged.

Not Mercurio.

Tess wore a shimmering, diaphanous emerald dress that flattered both her figure and her coloring. Her green eyes sparkled in the light. Her red hair tumbled down her shoulders, and her full, sensual lips were the color of raspberries against her pale skin. She looked like a star on the red carpet.

There was a gasp, a sudden whirl of paparazzi frantically taking pictures.

"What a beautiful dress, Princess! Is that from Mercurio's new spring collection?"

"Incredible!" another reporter shouted. "What a triumph!"

Slowly Tess turned to look at him, her eyes pleading. From the corner of his eye he saw their bodyguard collect her cape from the red carpet. Cameras flashed.

Stefano was frozen in shock.

His wife wasn't wearing a dress from Mercurio's new line. She wasn't wearing Mercurio at all—or Fortuna or any of the Gioreale brands. She wasn't even wearing Zacco.

He'd seen this exact dress in her suitcase. Seen her sighing over it once or twice, when she thought he wasn't looking. He knew exactly what it was.

This amazing dress was Tess's own design.

It was unheard-of to go rogue at an event like this. If you were an important guest of a fashion house's runway show, you always wore their clothes even if they were borrowed from the company. You wore them as a mark of respect, to play the PR game.

So what did it say that the CEO's new wife had snubbed the Mercurio brand to wear her own hand-stitched designs?

"Beautiful dress, Your Highness!" one of the reporters called to Tess. "So that's a preview of tonight's show?"

Tess blushed, looking more beautiful than ever. "No," she said shyly, "actually, it's—"

"It's her design," Stefano said, putting his arm around her shoulders. "My wife is an amazing new talent."

Tess looked shocked, but not as shocked as the reporters. Stefano knew, in supporting Tess, he'd seem to be insulting his own company and his new designer. Not only was Tess wearing her own clothes, but Stefano was outright promoting them on the red carpet instead of Mercurio's!

But what choice did he have? He set his jaw. How could Tess have put him in this position? How could she stab him in the back, injuring Mercurio's reputation when everything was on the line?

Reporters surged breathlessly forward. "Prince Stefano, are you saying—"

"Is Caspar von Schreck's job in jeopardy, Your Highness?"

"Is the spring collection a disappointment?"

Baring his teeth in a smile, Stefano said, "We're very proud of Mercurio's spring line. And tonight, you'll see it for yourself. That's all. Thank you."

Gripping Tess's arm, he walked her down the red carpet, not letting her stop for any other shouted questions.

"Thank you, oh, thank you, Stefano," Tess whispered. She took a shuddering breath. "I was so scared what you'd say, but I couldn't wear those dresses, I just couldn't—"

"How could you, Tess?" he said under his breath. "The press think I am snubbing von Schreck and trying to launch you as a designer!"

She sucked in her breath. "So why did you support me?"

"The alternative was to let them think we were already having problems in our marriage. I had to act proud of you!"

"Act?" She turned pale. "You mean you're not?"

Stefano ground his teeth. "You're talented, Tess. No one can dispute that. Your dress—" his eyes traced over her curves "—is spectacular."

Her eyes lit up. "Then—"

"But you can't seriously want to launch your own company. Do you want to work eighty-hour weeks in a studio, leaving Esme with a nanny? Do you know what it's like for a child to be raised that way? Because I do."

Her jaw tightened. "Have you forgotten I've spent most of Esme's life working flat out at my uncle's bakery?"

"No. I haven't," he said grimly. "Nor have I forgotten the reason. Because I abandoned you without financial support." Just thinking of how he'd left Tess and Esme destitute still made his stomach clench. "As long as you are my wife, you will have a comfortable life."

"What if I don't want to take it easy?" she retorted. "What if I want to follow my dreams?"

"What dreams? Being 'an assistant to an assistant,' as you charmingly put it, working endless days fetching coffee, doing very little design, for almost no pay?" he said scorchingly. "That's your big dream, instead of caring for our daughter?"

Tess's expression fell as they walked through the crowded foyer of the *palais*. "If I could find a way to do both..."

"Tonight the story was supposed to be Mercurio," he ground out. "Instead, now it will be you."

She looked abashed. With quiet defiance, she lifted her chin. "I couldn't wear those dresses, Stefano. They were horrible. No woman alive would want to wear them."

Her simple, obvious statement made his heart stop.

Tess was right.

Stefano couldn't imagine Caspar von Schreck's

beige, peculiar dresses on any woman of his acquaintance. What did that mean?

It meant that the new collection would fail.

It meant the stock price would fall.

It meant Zacco was lost for good.

As they entered the enormous ballroom in the palace, where Mercurio's runway show would be held, Stefano forced himself to greet people, to act confident, as if he didn't already know the battle was lost. As he spoke to acquaintances, he gripped his wife's hand. He was relieved when the lights started to flicker, an indication that the show was about to begin.

They found their seats. For this one show, he'd wanted to sit in the front row. He looked around them at the cavernous space. Were those smoke machines?

Foreboding went through him.

A moment after they sat down, all the lights abruptly went off, turning the ballroom completely black.

For a moment, the hundreds of guests inside the *palais* were silent. He smelled smoke. Then dramatic electronic music began to thunder around them. A strobe light, high overhead, began to flash outrageous patterns against the smoke.

Pain rose to Stefano's temples, throbbing in time to the loud music and pulsing lights.

The first model started down the catwalk,

wearing a dress just like the ones von Schreck had sent them earlier. It did not look any better on the model than it had on the hanger. The dress's cutouts highlighted strange parts of the model's body—her lower belly, beneath her armpit and half her breast—making her look awkward and peculiar. The sickening beige color made the girl's face look so washed-out she almost looked dead.

It's a disaster, Stefano thought wildly. But at least he'd been prepared. At least things couldn't get worse.

Then they got worse.

Avant-garde was how the most charitable magazines described the Mercurio show later. More typical words to describe it were *epic fail* and *instant internet meme.*

The electronic music and flashing lights that added such drama to the darkness abruptly faded with a loud scratching squeal. The Hokey Pokey played on the loudspeakers, the old children's song sounding somehow threatening rather than playful. The first model disappeared, and new models started rapidly coming down the catwalk one by one, wearing large, cartoonish animal masks that completely covered their heads, as if to distract the audience from all the lumpy beige and greige dresses.

A hush fell across the crowd, then tittering laughter. Camera phones came up.

And that was even before a model wearing a lion mask, who probably couldn't see well through the huge fuzzy mane, tripped on her high heels and fell off the catwalk, landing on the lap of a senior editor of *Vogue Italia*. The other models kept walking as if nothing had happened.

Stefano felt his wife's gentle hand on his arm. She was watching him with worried eyes. He realized his hands had tightened into fists.

The show seemed to last forever. When it was finally over, Caspar von Schreck, the young, trendy designer whom everyone on the Gioreale board of directors had pleaded for Stefano to hire, came out wearing a full lumberjack beard, baggy tweed trousers and an open shirt. Holding his little dog against his chest, he waved at the crowd and bowed as if he had done something amazing.

He had, Stefano realized. With one stroke, he'd just caused Stefano to lose his chance at buying back the company that had been in his family for generations.

No. That wasn't fair. It wasn't von Schreck's fault. It was Stefano's. He should have insisted on seeing the designs in advance. He should have known that just because the designer was talented, it didn't also mean that he wasn't crazy drunk on his own vanity.

"Oh, my God," a socialite breathed behind them, turning to speak into her camera for social media. "Did you all see that? My Halloween costume is sorted!"

Stefano rose abruptly to his feet, his jaw tight, and headed backstage.

He already knew that the stock price would plummet tomorrow. Even though Stefano was Gioreale's CEO and primary shareholder, he'd still have to explain this disgrace to other shareholders and the media, and explain how, under his leadership, Mercurio had gone from stock loser to international laughingstock.

"Stefano—"

Behind him, Tess's voice was pleading, but he didn't stop for her. He couldn't.

There was only one person he wanted to talk to right now. And it would be all he could do not to talk with his fists.

Tess felt sick to her stomach as she followed Stefano backstage. This was the Mercurio fashion show?

Where was the fashion?

All she'd seen was a bunch of starved-looking girls, many of them younger than her cousins, walking in clothes that looked like ripped-up grocery bags, stumbling down the catwalk in ridiculous animal helmets. It might be called performance art; to Tess it was just silly.

This was the show her husband had so badly

wanted to be perfect. She glanced at Stefano's tight shoulders in his tailored black jacket as he strode ahead of her through the crowd. Although she felt badly for him, something told her that her sympathy would be unwelcome.

Backstage was a madhouse of stylists and models with racks of clothes and people everywhere.

An American reporter, the cohost of an influential morning talk show, stepped into his path, hovering with a live camera crew.

"Your Highness! Prince Stefano! May I get a comment? What did you think of Mercurio's spring collection?"

"We are, of course, very proud," Stefano ground out, "to have such a daring, avant-garde artist as our creative director. His vision is world changing."

Tess could see from her husband's taut jaw how he really felt about it, no matter the PR spin he was trying to put on it. Then she heard wild yelling and barking.

Turning, she saw Caspar von Schreck loudly berating a young woman. His little dog was barking, adding to the noise. The shamed girl stood in tears, holding the lion mask in her arms.

Tess recognized Kebe, the beautiful model Stefano had once given a ride home in New York. She was the model who'd tripped on stage, Tess realized. She barely looked older than her nineteen-year-old cousin Natalie.

"You *idiot*," Caspar von Schreck was screaming into her face, flecks of spittle flying. "You clumsy *clod*!"

"Please, Mr. von Schreck," the girl whispered. Her shoulders slumped. "It was an accident..."

"You ruined my show with your incompetence!" the bearded designer shrieked. "I'm going to make sure you never work in this business again!"

Tess moved without even realizing it. She stood between the tearful young girl and the world-famous designer.

The man's bloodshot eyes narrowed as he sneered at Tess. "And what do you want?"

Tess stuck out her chin. "You're the one who should never work in this business again, you horrible man!"

A gasp went through backstage, followed by a low, gleeful hiss. The designer's eyes widened as silence fell and everyone turned to watch.

Von Schreck glared at Tess.

"And who are *you*?" He looked dismissively over her shimmering green gown. "You didn't even wear Mercurio to the show. You are *nobody*!"

Tess felt suddenly calm.

"You're right," she said evenly. "I'm nobody. But I know good clothes when I see them, and the three dresses you sent us today were the ugliest clothes in *history*!"

"The three…" The designer's eyes widened. "Wait. Are you—?"

"And you must know it, because why else would you force these poor girls to wear animal helmets? You should be ashamed of yourself!"

A low current of malicious laughter went through the backstage area. The designer was obviously not well liked even among his own people.

The designer's eyes narrowed dangerously as he took a step toward her. "Shut up."

"How dare you bully everyone!" He'd probably been cruel to his underlings, she thought, just like the poor tearful girl behind her. Imagining someone being so mean to her cousins or her daughter, Tess glared at him. "You might be famous," she said, her back snapping straight, "but the truth is, you're nothing but a no-talent hack!"

Von Schreck gave an enraged growl, drawing his hand back, as if to hit Tess across the face.

But his arm was caught.

"Don't even think about it," Stefano said coldly. He threw the man's arm aside. "You're fired, von Schreck."

The designer's face went pale. "Fired?"

"I agree with everything my wife just said." Stefano looked at him. "Now get the hell out."

Caspar von Schreck sucked in his breath, his

cheeks red as he looked around them, at the live camera crew and the models recording the moment on their camera phones. He stiffened.

"You can't fire me. I quit!" The designer tossed his head, causing his beard to flutter like a flag. "Mercurio doesn't deserve my amazing talent." Looking around, he proclaimed loudly, "Last week, Fenella Montfort offered me a job at Zacco, and I'm going to take it! That's a real fashion house!" As his dog barked noisily in his arms, he added maliciously, "Didn't Zacco used to be *your* company, Your Highness?"

Stefano took a step toward him, his dark eyes glittering. "Get out."

"Good luck finding a designer half as genius as me!" With a final toss of his beard, Caspar von Schreck turned on his heel and left, his dog yipping back at them angrily.

Exhaling in relief, Tess smiled up at Stefano, feeling so proud of him her heart could burst. Turning to the tearstained young model behind her, she said, "Are you all right?"

Kebe nodded, her eyes big. "Thank you." She wiped her eyes. "You had no reason to take my side."

"I had every reason. You're my husband's friend." Tess shook her head. "And no one has the right to treat people that way!"

Feeling a jacket suddenly covering her own bare

shoulders, Tess looked up at Stefano. A strange emotion glowed in his dark eyes. He said quietly, "I'm glad you were here."

Her heart warmed beneath his glance.

Stefano glanced at Kebe. "Your mother will be heartbroken when she hears how you were treated. I'm sorry."

"Don't worry. I'll tell her how you both rushed to my defense." Kebe grimaced. "But first I'm going to change out of this hideous dress."

"Prince Stefano!" The American reporter was panting in her rush to stick a microphone into his face. "There's a rumor going around that you deliberately fired von Schreck so you could replace him with your new wife, though she has no fashion experience whatsoever… Any comment?"

Tess's eyes went wide with shock. "No, it's not true."

"He was fired for gross incompetence," Stefano said evenly. "And for abusing the staff. Mercurio will start fresh next season. Though my wife is amazingly talented, she's focused on raising our daughter. Thank you."

"Your Highness!" Other reporters and bloggers were already fighting their way through the crowds backstage.

Stefano grabbed Tess's hand. "Excuse us."

Holding her hand tightly, he pulled her away. The front of the *palais* was just as much of a madhouse. People were yelling things out to them and blocking their path, and everywhere Tess looked she saw camera phones recording them.

For the first time, she understood the need for bodyguards as Leon suddenly appeared to help clear a path through the crowds. She didn't exhale until they were safely in the back seat of the limo.

The chauffeur drove them away, with Leon sitting in the front seat beside him.

Stefano turned to her. "I'm glad you were here tonight, Tess." Reaching out, he cupped her cheek. "Thank you for what you did."

"What did I do?"

"The right thing," he said quietly. "No matter the cost."

The sparkling city lights glittered beneath the autumn drizzle as the limo flew through the Paris night. Taking her into his strong arms, Stefano kissed her.

A week later, Stefano rose wearily from his desk in his private office of Gioreale's Paris headquarters. It was almost midnight, and the building was quiet. Even Agathe Durand had gone home, at his orders.

Rolling his shoulders, he went to the wet bar and poured himself a drink. No ice, not water. Just Scotch. Taking it back to the window, he stood looking out at the cold October night.

The large window overlooked the modern, bright steel-and-glass buildings of La Défense, Paris's business district to the west of the city. The moon seemed frosted with ice crystals in the darkness.

Stefano felt like a fool. He still had no designer for Mercurio. The luxury brand was in free fall. Before, it had been merely unfashionable; now it was a joke.

As threatened, Caspar von Schreck had gone to work for Zacco. Stefano took a gulp of Scotch. He thought of how often in the past he'd casually stolen key employees from rivals. In this case, he suspected Fenella Montfort might get more than she'd bargained for.

Her first mistake, he thought. Much good may it do her.

Stefano felt restless. He paced two steps in front of the window, then took another drink. He didn't feel like himself, because Prince Stefano Zacco di Gioreale always won, and this wasn't winning.

He'd spent the last week doing damage limitation, reassuring the press and Gioreale's shareholders that the Mercurio disaster was trivial and the future was bright.

Stefano took one more drink, staring out at the frosty Paris night. Enough, he thought. He set down the unfinished glass.

He was going home.

Locking up his office, he bade *bonsoir* to the overnight security guards. When he left the building, he felt the shock of cold air against his skin. Autumn was almost over, he realized. Winter was nearly here.

He looked back at the Gioreale building. He suddenly longed to be done with it. All of it. Fashion. Shareholders. Crazy designers. He closed his eyes, imagining a soft, warm land of orange groves, with vineyards ripening in the sunshine.

Gioreale. He'd named his company after his title. It was also the name of his family's ancient castle in Sicily, as well as the nearby village, neither of which he'd seen since he was a boy.

It was strange that he suddenly missed it now. For most of his life, he'd thought of Gioreale as the lonely prison of his childhood, before his parents had sent him to an American boarding school at twelve. Why did he now yearn for that warmth, for the scent of lemons and the exotic spice of the Mediterranean Sea?

Getting in his Ferrari, he drove back to the 7th arrondissement lost in thought. He reached his elegant residential building and parked in the garage, then took the private elevator to the penthouse floor. He felt he'd barely seen Tess or Esme all week.

He arrived to find his luxurious, sprawling apartment was dark. Of course. They'd gone to bed. He set down his briefcase and hung up his coat. Through the windows, he saw the illuminated Eiffel Tower shining brightly in the night. Then, late as it was, that too went dark.

He noticed a single light gleaming down the hall. His wife was awake. Tess had waited for him every night, no matter how late, no matter how often he told her she should get her rest.

"You're back earlier than usual," Tess said, smiling. Hiding a yawn, she sat up in bed, setting aside her novel. "I'm so happy you're home."

Her green eyes shone up at him adoringly. As if she—

As if she—

No. Stefano turned away, not wanting to see the love in her eyes. He told himself it wasn't there. Tess would be too smart to love him, knowing it could only bring her pain. He said shortly, "You didn't need to stay awake."

"I don't mind." She gave him a wistful smile. "It's the only way I can see you."

Looking at her, he caught his breath. She was wearing his favorite silk negligee, her brilliant red hair tumbling down her shoulders. His eyes drank her in hungrily, down her swanlike neck to the open neckline of her negligee, with the top of her breasts peeking out. Leaning down, he kissed her, and the tension in his shoulders eased.

When he finally pulled away, she gave a satis-

fied sigh. Her eyes twinkled. "Now that was definitely worth staying up for."

He was tempted to press her back against the
bed and make love to her, without another word.
Instead, he sat down abruptly beside her. He pulled
off one expensive Italian shoe, then the other, tossing them to the floor.

"What would you think," he said slowly, "about
taking a vacation?"

"Like a honeymoon?"

Stefano blinked. "Honeymoon?"

"Don't get me wrong," she said quickly. "I loved
Milan and London. And Paris is lovely. It's just…"
She focused on the closed book in her lap. "So
much of your time has been spent promoting Mercurio and negotiating for Zacco and working in
your Paris office. It would be nice to have a little
time just…with us."

Stefano stared at her.

She was right, he realized. They hadn't had a
honeymoon, not a real one. He'd spent the last
three weeks dragging her all over Europe, con-
sumed by things that didn't matter, things that had
all come to nothing.

He looked away. "Sure."

"Oh, do you mean it?" She clasped her hands
eagerly. "Where?"

He knew he could suggest all kinds of places.
His beach house in St. Barts. A villa in the south

of France. A yachting trip around the coast of Sardinia. Exploring the autumn foliage of New England. The Greek Isles.

Instead, he heard himself say, "Would you like to see my castle in Sicily?"

Tess's eyes lit up. "You know I would."

"It's not glamorous. But I was raised there." He lazily twirled a tendril of her red hair. "You can see the sea. There's vineyards. A half-ruined village."

"Sounds dreamy."

He gave a low laugh. "I can't guarantee that. I haven't been back to Gioreale since I was twelve."

"Gioreale." Her eyes looked enraptured. "Like your title?"

"It's your title now, too," he reminded her. "Yes, the name is from the castle. And the village is also called Gioreale. But like I said…it's a ruin."

"I remember." She nodded solemnly. "Prince of ghosts."

He barely remembered saying that. But it was true. The last time he'd seen the village, through the back window of the car as his parents' chauffeur drove him to the airport where he would travel alone to America, Gioreale had looked desolate, the shops abandoned, the young people all gone.

Tess looked thrilled at the prospect of a visit. "When can we go?"

"Tomorrow." He hoped he wasn't making a mistake taking his family there. His childhood hadn't been a happy one. Still, Tess seemed overjoyed, and he wanted to get away from the world. What could be more remote than a half-ruined castle in the Sicilian countryside?

"Thank you," she whispered, putting her hand on his cheek, rough with five-o'clock shadow. "You're so good to me."

"Am I?" His gaze traced from her full lips to her bare throat. The strap of her lilac-colored negligee had slid down her shoulder. He kissed her bare skin, golden in the lamp's soft glow.

Tess's expression changed. Reaching up, she loosened his tie, tossing it to the floor. Then, with a sensual smile, she switched off the lamp so the only light in the bedroom was the silvery moonlight cascading through the translucent window curtains.

Desire rushed through him, and amazement. Tess had never initiated lovemaking before. He kissed her hungrily, pushing her back against the enormous bed.

His hands ran roughly over her silk nightgown, and the even softer silk of her skin. He kissed her with all the passion in his soul, determined to make her body sing. And as he did, he tried to ignore the way his own heart threatened to come alive.

CHAPTER EIGHT

TESS SIGHED WITH PLEASURE, closing her eyes as she turned her face to the warm Sicilian sun.

The wind blew through her hair as Stefano drove the vintage red convertible. Her hair was pulled back with a scarf, and she was wearing a sundress and sandals. From the front seat of the car, she glanced back, smiling as their baby cooed happily from her car seat.

As soon as they'd arrived in Sicily on Stefano's smallest private jet, Tess had felt free, like they'd left all their troubles behind, along with their bodyguards, assistants and even the trusted nanny. Stefano's suits had disappeared, and he wore a casual black T-shirt and jeans that seemed to caress his powerful muscles. It was a different world.

Leaving the airport behind, they'd driven through the small city of Ragusa, where she'd goggled at an old mansion with stone faces carved into the balconies.

"The Palazzo Zacco," he'd told her.

Her eyebrows rose almost to her hairline. *"Zacco?"*

He snorted. "Don't get excited. It's not ours. It

was built by a totally different family. No—" he'd looked up, switching the car's gears with a grin "—our little place is up in the hills."

They'd traveled the slender coastal road on the edge of the cobalt blue sea. Now they were going deeper into the island, past orange and olive groves. As the road climbed up the hills, they passed vineyards heavy with the last grapes waiting for harvest. In the distance, she saw a village tucked into a small valley.

"The village of Gioreale," he said quietly. "Half destroyed by an earthquake in 1961. My father ruined the rest by neglect." As they drew closer, his hands tightened on the steering wheel, as if he were bracing himself.

But as they entered the village, Tess looked incredulously at the well-kept charming pink stucco buildings and freshly painted green shutters. There was a profusion of flowers, and the cars parked on the streets were gleaming and new.

At the center of the village, near a small, well-maintained church, outdoor cafés lined a square filled with tourists taking pictures of the lavishly sculptured stone fountain.

"I thought you said it was a ruin," Tess breathed as the convertible slowed. "A ghost town."

Stefano was staring around with amazement that exceeded her own. "It was." Blinking hard as if he didn't believe his own eyes, he looked back at it through the rearview mirror. "The fountain—did you see that? It had water! It never did before."

Tess tilted her head. "So it's changed since you left?"

"Yes…" Stefano's eyes widened. "But I never thought…" Not finishing the thought, he pressed on the gas. The red convertible flew up the next hill, as, in the back seat, Esme giggled and clapped her hands, clearly relishing the wind on her face.

Tess smiled back at her baby, then looked out at the rolling hills and took a deep breath of the fresh, fragrant air.

"It's more beautiful than I ever imagined." She held her hand out, in the direction of the sheep placidly grazing in a nearby field, and felt almost like she was flying. She looked at him. "I can't believe I'm princess of this magical place."

"Magical is right." Shaking his head, he gave an amazed laugh. "*Tourists*. In Gioreale."

Leaning back against the soft leather seat, Tess closed her eyes. She tried to remember the last time she'd felt so happy. The drama of Paris already felt like a world away.

Stefano had told her that his company's stock price was down nine percent. Costing him hundreds of millions of euros.

Costing him Zacco.

Which wasn't to say Mercurio hadn't gotten lots of press. It had mostly just been negative. The story was everywhere, first of the runway show itself, with the models in animal masks, capped by poor Kebe tripping and falling into the audience; then of the aftermath. The video of Tess chewing out Caspar von Schreck had already been viewed a million times. Many people were calling her defense of the young model admirable, but a good few had been insulting and rude, asking how a mere *trophy wife* had the right to attack a *true artist* like von Schreck. The one thing everyone agreed on: Mercurio might not survive this disaster.

It was all so horrifying that Tess had quit social media entirely. On the flight to Sicily, she'd called Hallie and Lola. Her friends had both been indignant on her behalf.

"Some bully was yelling at a girl? Of course you had to say something," Hallie said.

"You can't let bullies win," Lola had said, her voice oddly restrained.

Tess had been happy to hear her friends' voices. Stefano had spent much of the flight pacing, speaking tersely to shareholders and board members from Buenos Aires to Berlin. Grimly he'd laid down the law: no new clothing would be manufactured or shipped out until they'd found a new designer. It would be a crushing blow for their business, especially the flagship boutique in New York.

But they'd left that all behind. In the convertible, Tess glanced at Stefano out of the corner of her eye. He was so handsome, and never more so than now.

Golden sunlight frosted the edges of his strong features, his black eyes and olive-toned skin. His square jawline was already dark with five-o'clock shadow, though it was only noon. His short dark hair waved in the wind as his hands gripped the steering wheel.

How would Stefano feel if he lost Mercurio, on top of Zacco?

She couldn't bear to think of it. Not when he meant the world to her. Not when she…

"Look." He nodded forward. "The *castello di Gioreale*."

Following his gaze, she gasped.

At the top of the hill was an old fortified castle, surrounded by vineyards and lit up by sunshine.

"Wow," she breathed. Not only had he made her a princess, but he'd brought her to his castle, just like a fairy-tale prince. All her childhood dreams were coming true.

Especially this. Especially him. Looking at Stefano, her handsome prince, a lump rose in her throat. He was an incredible lover. An amazing husband. A wonderful father.

He could have been angry at her—for causing the scene with von Schreck, and for wearing her own design on the red carpet. Instead, he'd supported her. He'd announced proudly that the dress was Tess's own design. He'd protected her from von Schreck when the man had tried to hit her. And then he'd brought her here. Tess looked at him, her heart in her throat.

Dust kicked up around them as Stefano drove the vintage red convertible behind the castle. Stopping the car, he got out and rolled up a garage door, then drove into a stable that had been converted into a six-car garage.

"No wonder it's not locked." Turning off the gas, he looked around. The converted stable was mostly empty inside, with only a few old estate cars. "My father used to fill this with his Ferraris." He gave her a smile that didn't meet his eyes. "Let's see what else has changed."

Lifting their baby out of the car seat, Tess waited as he took three small suitcases from the tiny trunk of the convertible. Then she followed him out of the garage.

Outside, the stone castle was sprawling and magnificent. Manicured gardens stretched to the edge of endless vineyards, broken up by pretty clusters of trees. Far below, at the bottom of the hills, she could see the smoky blue haze of the sea.

Tilting back her head, she looked up at the castle in awe. Red bougainvillea climbed the walls like scarlet flames. Tears filled her eyes.

"What do you think?" Stefano said quietly.

Turning to face him, she tried to smile, holding their baby on her hip.

"I love it," she whispered. She lifted her tremulous gaze to his. "I just can't believe it's real."

He grinned. "Oh, it's real, all right. As you'll discover once you actually live in it. The castle was built in the late Middle Ages, but the foundations are much older. It was a palace in the days of the emirate."

"Emirate?"

"Sicily was the crossroads of the Mediterranean. Everyone's had a piece of it at one time or another. Ancient Greeks, Romans, Vikings, Arabs, Normans, Spaniards. And now Italians." He shrugged. "Conquerors come and go. My own ancestors came to Sicily six hundred years ago, in service to the king of Aragon."

It all sounded very romantic to Tess. She imagined the clash of swords between knights, a damsel languishing in a rose-covered bower. "It sounds lovely."

He gave her a strange look. "Lovely?"

"Romantic."

He snorted. "That's one way of looking at it, I suppose." Gazing up at the castle, he said, "I haven't been home in a long time."

"Everyone will be so excited to see you!"

"They all hated my father." He lifted their suitcases higher against his shoulders. "I doubt they'll be glad to see me."

The back door of the castle was unlocked. Inside, it was dark and quiet. Tess craned her head. The closest she'd ever been to the inside of a castle was the time she'd visited the Cloisters, the medieval museum in northern Manhattan.

She looked down at her feet. Even the floor appeared ancient, with a worn, colorful mosaic that looked almost Byzantine. Everything was old. The walls were rough stone, and the furniture was obviously hundreds of years old. There was actually a suit of armor in the hallway.

Above them, the ceilings were shadowy and dark, with few windows and thick stone walls. The temperature seemed to drop.

"This is what a real castle feels like," Stefano said, observing her with a grin.

"Amazing," she said, shivering.

"Don't worry. There's a modern wing that's a little more livable. This way."

It was funny, she thought. For all her life, since her mother had read her fairy tales as a child, Tess had dreamed of castles. As a student, she'd pasted pictures of famous castles on the cover of her writing notebooks. From a distance, the castle of Gioreale had indeed looked majestic and awe-inspiring.

As she walked through the windowless hallways, she was forced to face the hard truth that old castles were indeed dark, cold and uncomfortable inside. Sometimes, it seemed, reality was not nearly as good as the fantasy.

But sometimes... Tess looked at Stefano's broad shoulders as he walked ahead of her, carrying their luggage. Sometimes it was even better.

"In here," Stefano said, pushing a thick oak door open. Following him, she gasped.

They were in a traditional great hall, with a fireplace as tall as Stefano. The high ceiling had exposed beams and was painted with old family crests and insignias. There were windows, and the furniture looked comfortable and new. Well, comparatively new. Golden light flooded in from lead-paned windows overlooking the cloistered courtyard.

"The modern wing," he said.

"Modern?" she said faintly.

"Sì." He grinned. "It's only three hundred years old."

"Only!"

Setting down their luggage, Stefano looked at the crackling fire in the fireplace. "It's strange we haven't seen any of the staff. Maybe they're in the kitchen."

With Esme in her arms, Tess followed him down a different hallway, then another. Finally he pushed open a door. Inside was a gleaming kitchen—far more modern than three hundred years old—filled with people. They were all bustling about, preparing food.

A woman gave a shocked cry as a dish shattered against the tile floor.

A short white-haired woman pushed through the crowded kitchen. Her wrinkled face lit up as she stared up at Stefano in shock. With a cry, she threw her arms around him. Tenderly he hugged her back, speaking in rapid Italian.

Stefano finally pulled away, looking a little sheepish, but happy for all that. "Tess, I'd like you to meet Gerlanda, my old nanny. She's now housekeeper here." He looked down at the white-haired woman, now wiping her tears with an apron. "Gerlanda, I'd like you to meet my bride from America, Tess, and our daughter, Esme."

The elderly woman's eyes went wide, and then she gave a joyful cry. Turning back to the others, she said a few quick words in a strange dialect of Italian—Sicilian?—and all the others began to exclaim joyfully as well. Tess found herself surrounded by smiling people, all patting her shoulder and stroking the baby's head, welcoming her in English, in Italian or just by the warmth on their faces.

"Thank you, thank you." Gerlanda shook her hand joyfully at Tess. "For bringing him here."

Tears were streaking her kind face. "Welcome, my princess."

Awed by all the raucous, noisy delight now filling the gleaming kitchen, Tess turned to look at her husband.

They all hated my father, he'd said. *I doubt they'll be glad to see me.*

From the happy shouts and tears, she saw he'd been completely wrong.

"What are you all doing here?" Stefano said, looking at the platters of food being assembled on the marble counter. "Is there a party?"

The others burst into laughter and a cacophony of Italian and Sicilian.

"The festival of harvest," one of them explained, glancing in Tess's direction. She realized they were speaking in English so she'd understand and was touched at their kindness.

"It will be our biggest one ever, since we also celebrate the success of the winery."

"It's doing well?" Stefano sounded mystified. The people around him laughed, their faces in broad smiles.

"Our Moscato—it just got the top rating from a famous wine critic."

"The bottle price, it will go very high."

"Extremely high."

"More tourists will come to Gioreale. More hotels to open, more restaurants, more everything," another said happily.

"The harvest festival is this afternoon," a young woman said. "Please, you must come!"

In the corner of her eye, she saw Stefano hesitate. He glanced questioningly at Tess.

"Please, Princess, make him come!" a girl pleaded. "And your sweet baby."

"Of course we'll come," Tess said, smiling at them.

Everyone cheered. Speaking in rapid Italian, Gerlanda pulled off her apron.

"But you have traveled far. You must be hungry. Your bags are inside? Salvatore," she snapped her fingers, speaking to a nearby man. The man immediately left the kitchen, smiling as he passed them.

Gerlanda turned back, cooing at the baby. "I will make you some lunch. Just to tide you over."

"We're not terribly hungry," Tess began. She was still full from the lovely breakfast that Louisa had prepared them on the private jet.

"Of course you are," the Sicilian housekeeper said briskly. "You are too skinny. You must keep up your strength! For Stefano! For Gioreale! And this sweet little one." She stroked Esme's dark curls. "The festival is hours away. You will starve. I will bring you food."

Tess tossed her husband a pleading glance.

"Thank you, Gerlanda," he interceded. "But I'd like to show my new bride around the estate. And perhaps," he said thoughtfully, "visit the winery."

"Yes!" The older woman's face lit up. "See what you have done for us."

"What has Stefano done?" Tess said.

"After his father died, Stefano always made sure to send money for the village. Even when his company was small and he had nothing. He always sent it to us. Always." Her eyes gleamed with tears as she looked up at him. "Now you are here, so you can see your sacrifice was not in vain. Or your belief in us." Abruptly she turned away. "You are not hungry, fine, so I will make you a picnic."

Stefano stared after her with a smile tracing his lips. "Same old Gerlanda."

"She calls you by your first name," Tess said wonderingly. "No one else does. Not even your assistant."

"Gerlanda was my nanny for two years, from the time I was eight until ten." His smile lifted to a grin. "I think in her mind, I am still ten years old."

"If she loved you, why did she leave?"

The smile dropped. "She didn't. My mother fired her. She always got rid of any servant I started to care about. She didn't want me to get too attached to them."

Tess stared up at him in disbelief. "What?" she

breathed. "Your parents abandoned you—then wouldn't let you love any of your caregivers?"

"Not just caregivers." His voice was casual, but she saw the tightness around his eyes. "Anyone I loved would disappear. After Gerlanda was forced to leave, I made friends with kids in the village. But at the end of the summer, they were told not to play with me or their parents would lose their jobs. So I roamed over the countryside with the gardener's dog." He paused. "My parents thought it was vulgar. So they told the gardener to get rid of his dog. When he refused, he was fired."

"Oh, Stefano," Tess choked out, her heart breaking. How could anyone be so cruel, to systematically and deliberately remove all love from their own child's life?

"It's all in the past." Stefano's expression was cool. "I haven't thought about it for years." He took her hand. "Come."

But was it really in the past? As he showed her around the sprawling castle, Tess felt sick.

Because now she knew and could no longer deny it.

She loved him. She was totally and completely in love with her husband.

And he'd warned her against it from the start.

You know I'm not good with...with feelings, right? Emotions? I like you a lot, Tess. Especially in bed. But that's all I'm capable of. I just... I'd never want to make you unhappy or break your heart.

Loving Stefano, was Tess making the same mistake her mother had made—giving herself to a man who was totally unobtainable?

Had she just made the biggest mistake of her life?

"What do you think? Can you handle it?"

Tess jumped guiltily. "What? What do you mean?"

Smiling, Stefano took the baby from her, cradling Esme in his strong arms. "The castle. It's not too rustic for you?"

"Oh." She looked around the master bedroom. One of the staff—Salvatore?—had already brought up their three suitcases. She studied the twisted wood columns of the massive four-poster bed, and caught the view of the valley past the balcony. She tried to smile. "I think I can handle it."

But could she?

When they went back downstairs, they found Gerlanda waiting with a picnic basket. "And one of the village mothers thought you might find this useful for your walk."

Stefano looked doubtfully at a fabric contraption in the housekeeper's hand. "What is it?"

"A baby carrier!" Tess exclaimed. She'd wanted one for ages, but hadn't had the money. When she started to put it on, Gerlanda stopped her.

"It's man-size. For the father."

Tess turned to Stefano with a huge grin. "Even better!"

For the next few hours, they explored fields and vineyards, beneath the wide blue sky and golden light. Stefano held Tess's hand and carried their baby on his back. As Stefano pointed out interesting features of the estate and Esme jabbered behind them softly, Tess looked down at her hand wrapped in his larger one and felt tears in her eyes.

Stefano stopped abruptly. "What is it? What's wrong?"

She tried to smile. "Nothing. I'm just happy."

"So happy you're crying?" he said suspiciously.

"We're a family," she whispered, looking up at him.

Their eyes locked, and for a moment he looked stricken.

Then all trace of emotion was shuttered from his handsome face. "Of course we are." His voice was cool. He dropped her hand. "Ah. There's the winery."

Inside the squat, prosperous gray stone building, they found the winery staff busy serving the tourists in the tasting room, selling them bottles by the case. Seeing Stefano, one of the employees immediately took them back to the production area, where they found the vintner, a middle-aged man, looking harried amid all the vats.

The employee went ahead and quietly spoke in the man's ear. The vintner whirled and saw Stefano, and his face lit up. With a joyful clap, he strode forward and eagerly shook Stefano's hand, bowing again and again. Turning to Tess, he welcomed her with an embrace, a kiss on each cheek and a rush of words in Sicilian.

They spoke for an hour with the vintner and his staff, learning how the winery's production and fame had flourished and grown. Then Tess started to notice some of the tourists peeking into the production area and surreptitiously snapping photos—not just of Stefano, but also of Tess. For a moment she was bewildered, then she remembered that, back in the real world, she was all over social media right now, and probably TV, as well. Being even temporarily famous made her uncomfortable. She was relieved when they finally left the winery and returned to the castle's private land.

"The winery's doing well." Stefano sounded shocked. "I didn't realize. They're shipping all over the world. They can barely keep up production."

"You didn't know?" she said, surprised. "Don't you own it?"

"No, and that's probably why they're doing so well," he said dryly. "The village owns it, as a co-operative." He shook his head, a smile lifting up the corners of his lips. "All of Gioreale is thriving."

"Because you believed in them. Invested in them."

He frowned. "Of course I did. I grew up here. Who wouldn't?"

Your father, Tess thought, but she didn't say it. It wasn't her place. Family could be complicated, she knew. She didn't like to hear criticism of her own father, though he'd died three years ago without ever trying to contact her. Even after his death, she'd tried to respect his wishes—by not going to his funeral or ever telling his other family of her existence.

Was it right? Wrong? Tess didn't know. All she did know was that love could be complicated, and sometimes it could be hard to tell it apart from hate.

Which must be, she thought with a lump in her throat, why Stefano didn't want any part of it.

"I hope you're hungry," Stefano said suddenly, giving her a wicked grin. "If we don't eat this picnic, we'll never hear the end of it."

He led her to a grassy spot on the top of the highest hill, not too far from the castle. They spread a blanket so the baby could play. Six-month-old Esme's idea of play was to try to clap her hands and catch her own feet, which always left her in a paroxysm of giggles.

Beneath the October sunshine, they spread out the housekeeper's picnic of fruit, sausages, cheese and freshly baked bread, and shared a bottle of the famous red Moscato the vintner had pressed on them. Beneath them, in the castle courtyard, they could see servants preparing tables for the harvest festival—hanging fairy lights, flowers and colorful decorations. As the afternoon waned, more villagers started arriving by foot and horse and car, all of them loaded down with food and wine.

"You're sure you want to go tonight?" Stefano said, tilting his head. "This is supposed to be our honeymoon."

"I want to go. It looks fun. The villagers love you," Tess whispered, her heart in her throat. She took a deep breath. "And so do—" She lost her nerve. Stuffing her mouth with grapes and cheese, she swallowed. "Yum."

"It's all grown on this estate."

"Delicious."

His dark eyes lit up. He murmured, "You're delicious."

Leaning over on the blanket, he kissed her, and she felt her body rise. They kissed for a long time in the warmth of the October sun, until twilight approached and Esme needed to get ready for bed.

Tess trembled, thinking how she'd nearly told him she loved him. What would have happened? The best case, she thought, was that he'd have said, *Thanks, but no thanks.*

Worst case: he'd be packing now to leave her.

That night, as they attended the harvest festival, surrounded by people who couldn't wait to thank Stefano for all he'd done for them, she tried to convince herself that she could keep the secret for the rest of her life.

She didn't need Stefano to love her.

It was enough that she loved him.

Wasn't it?

Sitting beneath the fairy lights at the center table, Tess watched one person after another tell Stefano how he'd changed and bettered their lives. She tried not to love him. But it was hard, which was to say, impossible. And it hurt.

Because she knew he'd never love her back.

After all he'd gone through, who could blame his heart for turning numb? To Stefano, love must feel like pain. She could hardly bear to think of him as a lonely little boy, neglected and abandoned. Even his dog had been taken away.

If only my love could heal you.

Tess's eyes widened as she straightened in her chair.

If only she could show him that love wasn't something to be feared, but embraced.

If she could show him that true love could last a lifetime…

When the harvest festival was finally over and everyone started cleaning up, Tess rose to her feet and found Gerlanda, to ask how she could help.

In response, the housekeeper gave a hearty belly laugh.

"You, do the cleaning? No. I forbid it. You do enough. You make our prince happy."

"Sí," another woman said. "We want Prince Stefano's happiness, after everything he's done." Turning away, she smiled. "And by the way he looks at you now, Princess, you make him very happy indeed."

Following the woman's gaze, Tess turned. Stefano stood on the other side of the castle courtyard. His black eyes looked at her hungrily across the crowd. Their eyes locked in the velvety Sicilian night.

He came forward, and took her hand.

"It's late," he said huskily. She shivered at the heat of his touch. "Time for bed."

He led her into the castle and up the stairs. Their footsteps echoed against the worn stone. He never let go of her hand, only pausing to check on Esme, sleeping in the nursery next door. Then he led her to the bedroom.

Silvery moonlight flooded the large window. Glancing out, she saw the full moon frosting the dark valley, reflecting against the black sea. Coming behind her, he gently rubbed her shoulders, pulling her back against his body. "Are you happy, *cara*?"

She turned in her arms. "Very happy."

How long could she hide her love for him? She was suddenly scared as she glanced toward the enormous four-poster bed. Once she was naked in his arms, feeling him deep inside her, she feared the truth would explode from her lips, and it might cost her everything.

He must never know. He could never know.

Unless...unless she could somehow heal him. Change him. Or was that just her foolish heart believing what she wanted to believe, instead of cold reality?

Lowering his head to hers, Stefano kissed her passionately. She sighed, lost in his embrace. But, as he started to lead her toward the bed, she nervously pulled away, pretending to be interested in the shelves of leather-bound books stretching up the opposite wall.

"So many books," Tess said awkwardly, touching their spines. "They all look so old."

"They are, I suppose. I'll show you the library downstairs sometime," he replied in a low voice, pulling her back into his arms. "Thousands of books, some of them a thousand years old."

Her jaw dropped. "A *thousand*?"

His sensual lips lifted into a smile. "I love how innocent you are. The smallest things impress you."

"A small thing—a great room full of books a thousand years old!"

Stefano shrugged. "Small."

"Then what on earth would you call *amazing*?"

Lifting his hand to her ponytail, he pulled out the tie, and her red hair came tumbling down the back of her cotton sundress.

"Having you in my bed," he whispered.

Lifting her reverently in his arms, he carried her to the enormous four-poster bed. As he lowered his head to kiss her, she felt a sea breeze come in through the open window, scented with jasmine and exotic spices from distant shores. She felt the roughness of his jaw against her skin as he whispered words like an Italian invocation and kissed down the length of her body. Slowly he removed her clothes, and then his own. He made her feel she was on fire, lit from within.

And through it all, with every beat of her heart, came the rhythm of the words she longed to say.

I love you. I love you.

But the last time she'd said those words, Stefano had left, intending never to return. Just because she'd said, *I'm already falling in love with you.*

Strange. At the time, she'd honestly believed her words. She'd thought she knew what love was.

Looking back, Tess realized she hadn't known at all. She'd just been in love with the idea of love, and dazzled by a romantic, sensual night with the most handsome, powerful man she'd ever known.

Real love was different.

It wasn't flowers or jewelry or poetic words. It wasn't the fairy tale of a grand wedding or becoming a princess in a castle. It wasn't even spectacular, mind-blowing sex.

Real love was quieter.

It grew when you weren't looking. From moments of laughter, of sharing. From small kindnesses. Like all the little things Stefano did that he thought she wouldn't notice, not just for her, but for others. For his employees. For his hometown. For their child.

Despite his attempts to hide it, she'd discovered his deepest secret. Stefano's title might be *Prince*, but in his heart, he was something even better.

He was a good man.

She knew him now, perhaps better than he knew himself. She knew him, and she loved him.

Did she dare tell him? Would that be foolhardy—or brave? Would her honesty ruin their fragile happiness? Or would it be the start of a life more joyful than either of them could imagine?

As Stefano held her in his arms that night, as she felt the weight of his body over hers and the soft Sicilian winds blowing in from the balcony against their hot skin, she felt tormented, even as she shuddered with pleasure beneath the slow stroke of her husband's hands.

Until, when he pushed himself inside her, making her cry out with ecstasy, she could take it no more. As he shuddered into her with a low roar, she gripped his shoulders and looked straight into his eyes.

"I love you," she whispered. "I love you, Stefano."

The next morning, Stefano woke with a strange feeling in his chest, finding he'd cradled Tess naked in his arms the whole night as they'd slept. A flash of vertigo went through him, leaving him woozy and sick.

I love you, Stefano.

He could still hear the tremble of Tess's voice last night, see the piercing emotion in her emerald eyes. He'd been deep inside her, his whole body shuddering with pleasure, but when she'd spoken the words, something had gone through him, something greater than joy. Overwhelmed, he'd kissed her, again and again as she'd softly wept.

"I was so scared to tell you," she whispered, pressing her cheek against his naked chest.

"Don't be scared," he'd said, his heart in his throat. And he'd found himself whispering love poetry in Italian he'd thought he'd forgotten. Since they'd arrived in Sicily, the prison of his childhood had become paradise.

He'd kissed her again, then held her until they'd both slept with their naked bodies intertwined.

And for that brief moment, everything had felt right to him.

Waking in the morning was different.

I love you, Stefano.

A chill went down his spine. A pounding anxiety formed at the base of his brain. He looked at Tess, cuddled against him beneath the blanket, her beautiful face tender, smiling in her sleep.

Stefano couldn't breathe.

He had to get out of here.

Jumping up, he went to the closet. Pulling on boxers and dark trousers, he grabbed a suitcase that Salvatore had unpacked for them the night before. He came back toward the wardrobe.

"What are you doing?"

He saw Tess watching him in the shadowy pink light. Sleepy as a kitten, she looked soft and adorable and it made the feeling in his chest tighten a little more.

"Getting dressed."

She yawned, stretching her arms. "Is the baby awake?"

"No, not yet."

He thought of how he'd quoted love poetry last night, and he felt sick. It didn't mean anything, he told himself. A man could not be held to account for what he might say in the arms of a beautiful woman.

But he knew what was really happening. Why

he'd slept in her arms last night better than he ever had before. And that he must not—could not—let it happen. Because the moment he relaxed, the moment he surrendered to emotional weakness, everything would crumble beneath his feet.

Stay in control, he ordered himself, clenching his hands at his sides. *You feel nothing.*

"Stefano?"

"I have to go," he said flatly.

"What?" She sat up in bed, looking shocked. "Go where?"

"I must return to Paris to start the search for Mercurio's new designer. And then London, to see if I can convince Fenella Montfort to sell her shares."

But even as he spoke, he knew there was no way to buy Zacco now. Not unless he sold everything he owned outright, and maybe not even then. The woman had made it clear she had no desire to sell.

But Stefano had to give Tess some reason for his departure, and he couldn't explain the real reason. Not when he barely understood it himself.

"Oh." Tess looked down at her body, still covered by the luxurious cotton sheets. She gave him a forced, cheerful smile. "I guess it was silly of me to think we could stay in Sicily forever. Of course not. You run a billion-dollar conglomerate. So when do we leave?"

"I'm leaving now." He paused. "You and Esme will remain."

"What?" She clutched the sheet higher, over her naked body that just hours before had been hot and tangled beneath his own. "No!"

"You will do as I tell you." He couldn't bear to look at her beautiful, anguished face. Turning away, he stuffed a few more things in his suitcase.

"This is because I told you I love you, isn't it?" Tess's voice trembled. "I knew this would happen! I knew it!"

Stefano looked away. Outside, he could see the hills leading to a pink horizon over the distant Mediterranean and, beyond that, Africa. Without a word, he pulled on a crisp white shirt and tucked it into his trousers. Sitting in a nearby chair, he laced up his black leather shoes.

"Please, Stefano," she whispered. "Just talk to me."

His stomach tightened, but he forced himself to face her.

Tess's hands were clasped, her thick black eyelashes fluttering against her pale cheeks.

Dawn broke, and sunlight flooded the bedroom from the east-facing windows, frosting Tess's beautiful face with warm golden light. As their eyes locked, he felt strangely vulnerable. And no wonder. He'd never revealed so much of his heart to any other living soul.

Just that thought made the world start to spin again and that sick feeling rise in his chest.

"I just have to go." He looked away. "I will return in a few days. When I do…" He set his jaw. "We'll talk."

"Stefano, don't go," she whispered. "Please."

Stefano felt a hard, rough twist in his chest at the pain in her voice. He crushed his feelings just as he'd been trained to do. Snapping the small suitcase shut, he kissed her forehead, then left without another word and without looking back.

CHAPTER NINE

IT WAS THE longest four days of Tess's life.

Four days of being alone in a remote Sicilian castle, being asked by the villagers and servants where Stefano had gone. Four days of eating alone in the great hall with only her baby for company. Four days of looking anxiously online for news of Stefano and discovering none.

And four nights of sleeping alone in their big bed, dreaming of him. Four mornings of waking up with a knot in her throat, her heart hovering between hope and dread.

Did Tess have any reason to hope?

I will return in a few days. When I do, we'll talk.

He could love her, her heart stubbornly argued. She'd seen the way he looked at her when she'd told him she loved him. She'd felt the way he kissed her, whispering words in Italian that sounded like music. She loved him. And she thought he could love her if he let himself.

But, for him, all love had ever meant was loss and pain.

She could settle for him not loving her, she told

herself on the first day. She could live her whole life without ever being loved, she told herself on the second. He couldn't help it, she insisted on the third.

But on the fourth…

Everything in Tess rose up in rebellion.

She thought of her mother, waiting eight years for a married man to leave his wife. She thought of herself, waiting over a year for Stefano to return to her, convincing herself that he was trapped on a desert island with amnesia.

This was her life. Her baby's life.

No more settling.

No more excuses.

Esme deserved better.

And, Tess realized with clarity, so did she.

If Stefano didn't love her and she stayed anyway, no matter how she tried to endure his coldness, eventually her love would turn to hate. What would their marriage be like then? A prison. For both of them.

What would that teach Esme?

Stefano had been nearly destroyed by his parents' selfish cruelty. Even Tess, unthinkingly, had followed her own mother's path when she'd let herself fall in love with an emotionally unavailable man like Stefano, who in spite of his warmth and goodness, seemed now as cold and unreachable as a distant star.

Tess had learned to give too much. Stefano had learned to be selfish. He put himself first. Tess and the baby were mere baggage. Whether he took her with him on his travels or left her behind on a whim, he expected her to be his accessory. He expected to be the boss.

Though my wife is amazingly talented, she's focused on raising our daughter.

She'd been a little hurt, but told herself it didn't matter. Because there was something she wanted even more than to be a designer. She wanted to be loved.

Now she knew she'd be neither.

Tess closed her eyes, suddenly wishing she was back in New York with her family and friends. Wishing she still had a job, even a poorly paid one, where she could earn money and self-respect, rather than being dependent on Stefano, when he didn't love her.

She'd told him she loved him, and after one precious night, when he'd held her so tenderly, he'd left her in the morning. He'd abandoned her.

Again.

This was unbearable, she thought. She couldn't let it go on.

Now, standing on the balcony in the cool October night, Tess stared at Stefano's terse message for the tenth time since she'd gotten it an hour before.

On my way home. I think I know how to make you happy. Talk more tonight.

What did it mean? Tess shivered. Was he going to tell her he loved her after all?

Hearing her baby babble, she glanced back through the open door toward the master bedroom, where Esme, fresh from her bath and in footsie pajamas, was playing with soft blocks on the bedroom rug.

Tess looked hungrily toward the pale sliver of road between the violet-purple hills leading to the castle. She expected Stefano any moment. She wrapped her arms around her body, hugging herself for comfort. She'd hoped he would arrive before the baby's bedtime, but it was almost too late…

Then she saw the headlights. A car was racing toward the castle at a breakneck speed.

She jumped, as if afraid of being caught waiting for him again. She hurried back into the bedroom, her hands shaking as she slid the balcony door closed behind her. Inside, her eyes caught her reflection in the full-length mirror.

Tess's pride hadn't been able to talk her out of trying to look nice tonight. Her wild red curls tumbled over her shoulders, and she wore a simple dress of her own design, with pink roses patterned on black silk. Spots of feverish pink color stood out on her cheeks.

"Bah!" Esme said proudly, holding up her chubby arms. The baby had recently figured out how to sit, but Tess always made sure to surround her with pillows for those moments when Esme would topple over with a crash.

"You have a block! Good job!" Tess picked the baby up, cuddling her close, relishing her sweet smell. She thought of why she'd married Stefano. So they could be a family. So they could be happy.

So they could love each other.

Please, let him love me, Tess thought, closing her eyes. *Please, let my faith be rewarded.*

She heard noises downstairs, as Stefano's deep voice called out to staff in Italian and they answered. With his return, the castle seemed to come alive.

Or maybe it was just Tess. She waited, practically vibrating, until she heard his heavy step in the hallway. Trembling, she turned to face the bedroom door.

Stefano's tall, broad-shouldered silhouette filled the space. He was wearing a well-cut suit and tie that perfectly fit his powerful, muscular body. His handsome face was serious. His dark eyes cut through her heart.

"Hello, Tess," he said quietly.

"Hello," she said, her heart pounding.

Coming forward, he kissed her softly on the cheek. She inhaled his scent of soap and spice and power. She felt the warmth and heat of him so close to her.

Please, she thought. *Please, please, please.*

"And Esme." His eyes crinkled as he smiled at her. Gently he took the baby in his arms, giving her a kiss before turning back to Tess. "How was she?"

"She missed you," Tess said. "So did I."

Stefano's handsome face suddenly became a mask. "It's past her bedtime."

"I let her stay up, hoping you'd get here."

"Thank you." His voice was courteous, impersonal. Tess bit her lip, feeling strangely awkward, as if she were speaking to a stranger, not her own husband.

Oh, this was ridiculous.

Biting her lip, she blurted out, "Stefano, you know we—"

"I'll put her to bed." Holding the yawning baby, he turned away, pausing at the door. "Gerlanda has arranged dinner in the great hall. I'll join you in a moment."

And he was gone.

Tess felt numb. For four days, she'd yearned for her husband's return. Now she felt afraid. What if her fears were right and her hopes were wrong?

I think I know how to make you happy, his message had said.

What could that mean, except that he was going to tell her he loved her? It had to be, she reassured herself. Straightening her shoulders, she went downstairs.

The great hall was newly decorated with vases of roses, reminding her with a pang of the roses on their wedding night. A fire crackled in the large fireplace, and shadows shifted across the exposed beams and painted ceiling above.

A small, intimate table for two had been set up beside the fireplace. Dinner had already been served and was waiting on china plates, beside linen napkins and sterling silver utensils. Nearby was a bottle of champagne on ice.

Seeing that, Tess exhaled with relief, her heart filling with joy. She knew instantly that everything was going to be all right.

Stefano loved her. That was what he'd come to tell her. Why else would they celebrate with expensive champagne?

All the pain she'd felt for the last four days—all the uncertainty and fear—disappeared in a puff of smoke. It had all been worth it, because now she knew he loved her, and—

"You look beautiful."

Hearing Stefano's voice behind her, Tess turned with a smile. "You're not so bad, either."

Shadows and firelight moved across the hard angles of his handsome face as he came forward. He pulled a black velvet box from the pocket of his black jacket. "I got you something."

"You didn't have to do that." *Just loving me is more than enough.*

"You deserve it." He opened the black box to reveal an exquisite diamond necklace, probably worth millions. He smiled when he saw her shocked expression. "Let's see how it looks on you."

Nervously Tess lifted her hair so he could wrap the expensive necklace around her throat. She shivered at the touch of his fingertips. Attaching the clasp, he stepped back to look at her.

"Beautiful," he whispered.

Numbly Tess reached up to touch the stones. She preferred the warmth of his hands. The diamonds felt cold and hard and heavy against her skin.

"Shall we have dinner?" he asked, gently putting his hand against her lower back to guide her.

He held out her chair, then sat down on the other chair across the small table. For a few moments, they ate the pasta without words. Tess felt the silence like a knife. Why wouldn't he just say it?

"I missed you," she blurted out.

"And I missed you." He paused. "I was wrong to leave you like that," he said quietly. "I'm sorry."

She exhaled. "It's all right. You're here now."

"Yes. And now," he said, his dark eyes smiling as he reached for the champagne bottle, "we celebrate."

"Celebrate what?" she said, her heart pounding.

After popping the bottle open, he poured two glasses and handed one to her. "I was a fool. I should have seen this long ago."

"What?" she almost shouted.

He was going to tell her he loved her. He was going to say it right now. And then everything would be all right. They'd be happy for the rest of their lives.

Stefano looked at her. He was so handsome, his eyes so dark and devastating, that just looking at him made her heart squeeze roughly in her chest.

"I want you to know," he said, and leaned forward, "that I've just managed to hire Aiko Sakurai away from Zacco as Mercurio's new creative director."

It was so unexpected it took her several seconds to even make sense of his words. She said weakly, "You did?"

"Yes," he said proudly. Reaching over the table, he took her hand in his own. "But there's more."

Thank heaven. Tess nearly cried with relief. For a moment there she'd actually thought—

"I'd like to hire you," he said. "As associate designer at Mercurio."

Her jaw dropped. Her heart fell to the cold gray flagstones.

"What?"

"You'd answer directly to Mrs. Sakurai, whom you admire so much. No fetching coffee. Just doing the design work you love." He beamed at her, then held up his hand sharply as if to ward off her protests. "I know you don't have any experience, and it's a big leap. But just think of what you can learn. Perhaps, in a few years, you could take over one of the smaller houses. Perhaps you can eventually take over Mercurio entirely. I have faith in you."

"But," she said through numb lips, "you said it would be ridiculous for me to work at a major fashion house. You said I'd have to work such long hours, and be away from Esme…"

"All my companies have on-site day care."

"I'd still be away from her for—how long did you say? Sixty hours a week?" Her voice trembled. "And away from you."

He shifted in his chair. "That won't be a problem, at least for a few months. I've decided to sell controlling interest in my conglomerate."

"What!" she gasped. "Sell Gioreale? All your luxury brands? Even Mercurio?"

He gave a single nod. "I'll need to sell my shares at top price. Then I can make Fenella Montfort such an offer for Zacco that only a fool would refuse."

"So," she said slowly, "I wouldn't be an associate at Mercurio for long, would I?"

His jaw set. "I'm sure the new CEO will wish for Aiko Sakurai to remain as creative director. She had global success at Zacco. She only left because she didn't want to work with von Schreck." He considered. "If she likes your work, she'll want to keep you on her team."

Tess shook her head. "You'd really sell the company you built with your own two hands? Just for your family's old company, with von Schreck as creative director? How can that be worth it?"

He stared at her, then turned away, his jaw tight. "I'll be traveling to get my company in order and ready for prospective buyers. In the meantime, you and Esme can go live at our apartment in Paris—"

"Without you. So I can have a possibly temporary job that no one will think I'm qualified for."

Stefano was still holding up his champagne flute, obviously expecting her to clink her glass against his in a toast to their future. At that, he set it down.

"I'm giving you what you want most," he said slowly. "Am I not? Arranging a job with a mentor you admire. Putting you on the path to becoming designer of a major fashion house. I thought you'd be thrilled."

Tess stared at him.

She couldn't believe she'd done this to herself *again*—twisting the bounds of reason to talk herself into believing what she wanted to believe.

He didn't love her.

He hadn't even tried.

Ice cut through her heart. She'd thought she knew him. In her mind, Prince Stefano Zacco was an honorable, dashing, scarred hero, Heathcliff and Mr. Darcy rolled into one. But the truth was that, throughout their marriage, as she'd made one compromise after another, sacrificing little fragments of herself for his sake, he hadn't done the same.

"I told you I loved you," she whispered, trying not to cry.

His jaw set. "And I told you, that's not something I can give you. I wish it were."

"You didn't even try," she said miserably.

Leaning forward, he grasped her hand over the table.

"I can't," he said quietly. "So just take what I can give you, Tess. Take it, and be happy."

For a moment, she looked at him, at this magnificent great hall in the Sicilian castle, surrounded by diamonds and flowers and silver and expensive champagne, a fire roaring in the fireplace.

All this elegance and grace, she thought dully. All something out of a fairy tale. A fashion magazine.

Once, she'd yearned to be part of this world. If

she stayed, if she agreed to his terms, she could be. All her childhood dreams could come true.

Except the one that really mattered.

Could she choose this beautiful, glamorous life, one that others would envy, when it meant she'd never be really, truly loved? Never ever, not until the day she died?

The answer thundered in her heart.

No.

Love was what she wanted. Real love.

And if Stefano couldn't love her, she had to be true to her own heart.

Pulling her hand away, she looked at him with tears in her eyes. She couldn't believe she was doing this. She choked out, "I can't."

Stefano appeared astonished. Then his black eyes glittered in the firelight. "Can't, or won't?"

Her voice shook. "What's the difference?"

His dark brows lowered like a thundercloud. He growled, "Then what the hell do you want?"

Tess looked at him and, with a deep breath, she made one final attempt.

"What I want," she whispered, "is for you to be brave enough to admit you love me, too."

It was suddenly quiet in the great hall. Stefano heard the crackle of the fire as logs snapped and burned. He heard the roar of blood pounding in his ears.

What I want is for you to be brave enough to admit you love me.

Stefano had spent the last four days running from her. He'd fled first to Paris, then London and Madrid. He'd done it to check on the efficiency of Gioreale's regional offices.

No. That was a lie. He'd been desperate to escape Tess's words. He couldn't let her love him. He couldn't love her back.

And, yet, he couldn't leave her.

Today at dawn, he'd had the solution. Giving Tess, who'd never even graduated from design school, an important job at Mercurio was a huge risk. But it was a risk Stefano was willing to take. He wanted Tess to be happy. To be fulfilled.

Just as he would be, after he got back control of Zacco. His family's company was his destiny. His future legacy.

What his father had lost, Stefano would win.

But he wanted Tess at his side—smiling, adoring Tess, so caring and kind. To keep her as his wife, he was willing to do almost anything.

But it hadn't been enough. His name, his home, his jet, his fortune, and even his fashion house—all not enough for her. She continued to demand the one thing he could not, would not give her.

What I want is for you to be brave enough to admit you love me, too.

Cold fury built inside him.

"You think I'm not *brave* enough?" he said, narrowing his eyes. "You're calling me a coward?"

A lesser woman would have quailed, retreated. Tess lifted her chin. "Yes."

He sucked in his breath, staring at her.

Tess was no longer the naive girl he'd married, he realized, the one with rose-colored glasses and pink-hued dreams. Her lips, formerly always so ready to smile, were now pressed together in a thin trembling line. Her green eyes, which had once danced with optimism and hope, were flat, as if all the dreams had been pulled out of them.

Because of him?

He wanted the old Tess back. He wanted them to be who they'd been. He wanted to mess up her hair, to see her smile, to see her face light up with joy as he lowered his head to kiss her. His jaw tightened.

"I can't give you what you want," he said in a low voice. "Why can't you understand that?"

"Why can't you change?"

Funny, he thought dimly. She'd been hoping all this time he'd change. He'd been hoping she wouldn't.

He said evenly, "Acquiring Zacco has to be my focus right now. Fenella Montfort is refusing to negotiate or even receive offers from my lawyers. It's going to take all my time and energy to convince her to even see me. I am trying to make you happy in my absence. Trying to—"

"I know what you're trying to do." Her eyes pierced his soul. "Buy me off. But I won't be part of it."

His dark eyebrows lowered fiercely. He growled, "Tess, damn you—"

"No."

Looking at her wan face, Stefano felt his heart twist. He suddenly wanted—

No. He fought the feeling, focusing on his anger.

"So what do you want me to do, Tess? Just stay here with you? Let Fenella Montfort keep Zacco? Surrender my family's name forever? Our legacy?"

"No," she said quietly. "What I want is for you to start a new legacy." She looked down at her hands. She was twisting her enormous diamond ring around her finger. "That company is not the only thing that bears your name."

She was talking about Esme, he realized. She and Tess also bore the Zacco name now.

Anger built higher. She was attacking him, and he had to defend himself. "I married you, isn't that enough? I've been a good father. I've given you both everything I can. Even you—I'm offering you a position that any other young designer would kill for!"

"I know," she said softly. "And I'm grateful."

That was more like it. He leaned forward. "Then—"

"But I don't want to be your employee. Only your wife." She blinked back tears. "I wanted so badly for you to love me, Stefano. I would have given everything—my heart, my soul—to make it come true." Reaching up, Tess unclasped the million-euro diamond necklace. "But I don't want this."

Gripping the jewelry in her hand, she held it out to him across the table.

"That necklace is a gift," he said, hurt. "I bought it for you."

"Take it back. Wait." He watched in shock as she pulled the diamond ring off her left hand and added it to the ball of precious jewels she extended toward him. "Take it all. I don't want it anymore."

Disoriented, he held out his hand, letting her drop the hard, cold diamonds into his palm.

"Not even the ring?" he said, his heart numb.

Her green eyes looked gray. "You don't love me."

"I never promised to love you. Just to honor and cherish. To romance you."

"I didn't know the difference then." She took a deep breath. "Now I do."

A roar of pain rushed through him, which swiftly turned to anger. Dropping the diamonds to the table with a clatter, he said, "If you're threatening to divorce me because I can't give you every single thing you want—"

"Every single thing?" she repeated incredulously.

"You're being unreasonable," he ground out. "What does love matter? It's just a word."

"Not to me." Anguished tears filled her eyes. "Please, Stefano. If you cannot love me, then please," she whispered, "let me go."

Let her go? *Let her go?* Every part of him rejected that ridiculous notion. She belonged to him! Tess was his wife. Esme was his child. They belonged with him. At his disposal. At his command.

He set his jaw. "No."

"You must." Her sad voice echoed in the great hall, beside the crackling fire. "If you don't let me go, it will destroy us both."

He stared at her. "You would throw our marriage away for nothing? Because I won't say those three words? Because I won't *lie?*"

"Because you're afraid."

"Afraid," he sneered.

She nodded. "I understand why, after everything you went through, but Stefano, don't you understand?" Shaking her head, she choked out, *"Loss happens anyway.* Whether you're brave enough to love or not. The answer isn't to feel nothing until we die. The answer is to seize our joy and *live.* To love as hard and long as we can."

Tears streaked openly down her face. "As I wanted to love you."

Stefano's jaw clenched as he stared at her. Did she think he was a fool? Of course he wanted to love her! He just did not know how! If he could have spoken three words as a magic incantation to make her happy forever, he would have!

But he couldn't feel them, and he couldn't lie and pretend he did. He wished he could. Stefano took a deep breath, trying to force the words from his lips. *I love you.* No one else found it hard. Why did he?

The words choked in his throat.

Savagery filled his heart as he turned away. Fine. He would simply lay down the law. He would tell her how it would be. She was his wife, damn it. She would remain so. She would obey—

Then he heard the quiet heartbreak in her earlier words. *If you don't let me go, it will destroy us both.*

He thought of the optimistic, romantic, dreamy-eyed girl she'd been. He looked at the heartbroken woman in front of him now.

When he'd married Tess, he'd honestly thought it was for her own good. He'd believed he could take better care of her than any other man.

He was no longer sure of that.

He said in a low voice, "I have given you everything I have to give."

"I know," she whispered.

Stefano rose unsteadily to his feet. He felt dizzy and powerless and cold all over, in a way he hadn't felt since he was a boy. He stared down at her.

"Go, then," he said hoarsely. "Take Esme and go."

Closing her eyes, she took a deep, shuddering breath. When she opened them, they were luminous with grief.

"Thank you." Rising from the table, she walked slowly up the stairs. Stefano stood by the enormous fireplace in the great hall, frozen in shock.

Surely Tess would come to her senses. Surely she'd realize that they were meant to be together.

But when she came back downstairs five minutes later, she was wearing a coat, with a diaper bag over her shoulder and Esme sleeping in her arms. "I saw Salvatore in the hall. He'll give me a ride to the airport."

Stefano looked at his wife and child, and his chest twisted painfully. He couldn't breathe. He didn't want them to go.

"Goodbye," Tess choked out. She turned to go.

"Wait."

She stopped, not turning around. Stefano still couldn't believe this was happening. He came up behind her.

"If you really love me," he said in a low voice, "how can you leave?"

Tess turned, and the look she gave him cut him to the core. Stefano realized her rose-colored glasses were finally gone. She now saw him exactly for the man he really was.

"I loved an illusion," she whispered, and left.

CHAPTER TEN

"You have some nerve. Stealing my designer."

Fenella Montfort softened her words with a feline smile. She was sitting behind her black lacquer desk in her office at London's Zacco headquarters.

"I didn't steal Aiko Sakurai," Stefano replied coldly. "She quit after you hired von Schreck to replace her."

"I intended for them to be co-designers. Creators of a brand-new synergistic vision."

He gave a grim smile. "Apparently Mrs. Sakurai didn't see it that way. Your loss. My gain."

"I still have von Schreck."

"Which is why you should sell all your shares now. Because once he shows his first collection, your numbers will drop."

Fenella narrowed her eyes. He returned her gaze coolly.

Stefano should have felt a thrill of triumph. For the last month, since Tess had left him, he'd focused on this goal, day and night. He'd done everything he could to get this meeting today.

His own company, Gioreale S.p.A., had already gotten offers from around the world for Stefano's controlling interest in the stock. He'd hired away Zacco's star designer, Aiko Sakurai, by tripling her salary and giving her a large amount of stock, so even if the company sold, she'd be wealthy enough to start her own brand, should she choose. And Fenella Montfort must by now have some inkling how awful Caspar von Schreck would be for Zacco.

For once, Stefano held all the cards.

And he would have traded every one of them, he thought, to have his family back.

Just thinking of Tess caused a deep ache through his body, from his throat to his jaw to his chest to his hips. All of him.

Turning away, Stefano looked out the large window, toward the gray steel and glass of London's business district, and behind that, the gray November sky. All so gray, Stefano thought. Flat and gray.

"So cheeky," Fenella said.

Taking a deep breath, he tried to focus on her. "So that's why you finally agreed to a meeting? Because I stole your designer?" Stefano knew she was as competitive as he was.

"Not just that," Fenella said. Clicking on her computer, she turned the monitor to face him on the other side of the desk.

A shock rippled through his body.

Tess's picture was on the monitor. He hadn't expected to see her. He'd spent the last month trying not to think about her, or think at all. Since she'd abandoned him so brutally, their only connection had been through his New York lawyers, working out a custody agreement for Esme. He'd tried to arrange for Tess to receive a generous monthly stipend, not required by their prenuptial agreement. To Stefano's shock, Tess had refused it.

Even his money, it seemed, was no longer good enough.

Tightening his jaw, he glared at Fenella on the other side of her desk. "Why are you showing me a picture of my wife?"

"Didn't you read it?"

Stefano looked closer at the screen. It was an online article from a New York newspaper.

It seemed he hadn't been the only one who'd been busy this past month. Since she'd returned to New York, Tess had already begun her own small fashion studio. Tonight, according to the article, she'd be hosting a charity runway show for her first capsule collection at the Campania Hotel.

Stefano looked back at the picture of Tess. His heart lifted to his throat. She was sitting at a bright green desk in a colorful bohemian office, with their sweet baby daughter playing nearby on a fluffy white rug covered with baby toys. Tess's beautiful face beamed up at him, her red hair tumbling down her shoulders, her emerald eyes warm.

So much light and color. She'd done it even without his help. She'd followed her dreams, on her own terms. He was proud of her, so proud.

Tess had never really needed him, he realized. She'd always had the strength to pursue her dream of being a fashion designer. Why had she ever been willing to accept less?

Because of him.

I don't want to be your employee. Only your wife. I wanted so badly for you to love me, Stefano. I would have given everything—my heart, my soul— to make it come true.

But he couldn't love her. So she'd left him. She'd started her own small business. A company with integrity. With heart.

Just like Tess.

She was better off without him.

Stefano was filled with grief he hadn't felt for a long, long time.

Without looking up, he said in a low voice, "Why did you show me this?"

"This is really why I invited you," Fenella said. "Not because of Aiko Sakurai—at least, not *only* because of her." Her cool eyes met his. "But because your wife has left you."

Stefano looked up sharply. "So?"

"That makes you interesting."

"How?" His lips twisted bitterly. "You sense weakness?"

"I sense strength." Tilting her head, Fenella said, "The possibility of a partnership."

Partnership. At the word, Stefano felt overwhelmed with memories of the partnership he'd had with his wife. The two of them laughing, talking, making love. Supporting each other. Caring for their baby. Pain went through his heart.

"What are you talking about?"

Leaning forward, she said coolly, "We have an opportunity."

"You're finally willing to negotiate for Zacco?" he said, leaning back in his chair so he didn't gag on the overwhelming floral smell of her perfume.

"Now that your unfortunate wife is gone—"

"Don't call her that—"

"You should replace her. With someone more appropriate."

Fenella's cold blue eyes met his, and he knew exactly whom she was suggesting.

A chill went through him. He rose to his feet, pacing to the window. He looked down at the gleaming steel and glass buildings beneath the lowering November sky. He finally said, "Are you trying to imply you care for me? Because we both know that's a lie."

"I care about success. And so do you." She rose to her feet. "We come from the same world, Stefano. Our families go back generations. We both know how to win—at any price."

A ray of sunlight burst through the gray clouds, illuminating the faint web of lines around her hard blue eyes.

"Forget love." She shook her head. "Love is for losers. You and I—we were born to rule. If we join our companies together, we'll be more successful than you can imagine. We have no limits. We can work twenty hours a day, every day, until we achieve it. We'll be so powerful, no one will ever be able to touch us." She took a step forward. "The world is ours to take."

Stefano stared at her.

Fenella Montfort was offering everything he'd once thought he wanted. Thought he needed. The pure control of single-minded focus that led to absolute power.

Wasn't that what he wanted—to never feel vulnerable again?

Tess had been right, he suddenly realized. He had been afraid. Of being powerless. Of feeling the pain of loss. So he'd pushed her away. Refused to love her.

Then why was it, that from the moment Tess had left, all he'd felt was the abyss of howling, terrifying loss?

His eyes went wide.

Loss happens anyway. He heard the echo of Tess's voice. *Whether you're brave enough to love or not. The answer isn't to feel nothing until we*

die. The answer is to seize our joy and live. To
love as hard and long as we can.

"Well?" Fenella purred as she came closer.
"What do you say? Do we have a deal?"

With an intake of breath, Stefano looked up at
the woman's cold, calculating gaze. If not for Tess,
he might have accepted her offer. He might have
given away his only chance of real happiness for
the sake of power and fortune.

But power was an illusion. Fortune was empty.
He knew that now. Because for the last month,
without his wife and child, he'd felt nothing. Everything he'd once cared about was worthless. A
booming stock price. Unimaginable wealth. Why
did he need more of those things when they didn't
make him happy?

Love was the only real legacy.

He closed his eyes, remembering Tess's quiet
voice. *Start a new legacy,* she'd said.

He hadn't understood it then. Now he remembered days of warmth and joy, of red wine and
sunshine and blue skies. Nothing to do with money
or power. A different kind of legacy.

He opened his eyes slowly.

Love.

Suddenly he had to see Tess. Now. Immediately.
He felt dizzy with need. He needed her like sunlight. Like rain. Not because she loved him, but
because he loved her.

He loved her.

Stefano looked at Fenella. "Not interested."

Her eyes narrowed. "Don't be a fool."

A beam of sunlight fell against his cheek, warming Stefano like the touch of Tess's hand, and he suddenly knew he was throwing away everything he'd once wanted for everything that truly mattered. He understood now.

Tess.

A smile rose straight from his heart. "Keep Zacco. I don't need it. I already have everything any man could dream of."

Stefano felt free. Joy thrummed through him like a song. Like a whirl of color. Red like Tess's hair, green like her eyes, their baby's laughter calling to him across the sea. "Goodbye, Ms. Montfort."

Grabbing his coat and briefcase, he strode out of his office, glancing back one last time at the Zacco headquarters. He knew he'd never see it again.

For all his adult life he'd thought winning the company was the only way to save the family legacy. To save himself.

Tess had shown him otherwise.

Life wasn't a game to be won or an asset to acquire. It wasn't a business based on profit or loss.

Life meant giving your heart. Taking the risk. Because though loss was guaranteed, joy was a choice. And joy came only from loving others.

Love was a gift, freely given. A leap of faith in this cold modern world. It wasn't weakness. It wasn't illusion. It wasn't even an ocean to drown in.

Love was the life raft.

"I never should have agreed to this," Tess breathed, raking her hand through her untidy red waves. "Why did I think I could do this?"

Her two friends looked at each other.

"Because you can," said Lola firmly.

"Easy," said Hallie.

Tess's first runway show was due to start in five minutes, in the intimate venue of the hotel's elegant Edwardian tearoom. They were in a back-stage area with the models and mirrors and racks of clothes. Their three babies were being watched by Cristiano and Tess's cousins.

Looking at her now, Hallie gave a low laugh, then covered her mouth with her hand. "Sorry. But you look so nervous." At Tess's glare, she added with a grin, "I'm just remembering how it felt. But you guys still made me go onstage and sing!"

"Because you're amazing," Tess said.

Hallie looked at her pointedly. "And so are you. Which is why I invested in your brand."

Tess's *brand*? She had a brand? All she'd done was design clothes she liked. But Hallie was right. She had a brand now. The thought made her want to run back to cower in the Morettis' old hotel suite upstairs, where Tess had been staying with Esme since Hallie's family had moved into their remodeled mansion in the West Village. "I never should have let you invest in my company, Hallie. I'm not ready!"

"Of course you are." Lola looked at the models around them, each of them carefully dressed in an outfit that Tess had designed and sewn herself. "Your clothes are so pretty." She looked down at her own outfit, also a Serena original. "And shockingly comfortable!"

"We're going to make a bundle," Hallie said gleefully, rubbing her hands together. "I can't let Cristiano be the only entrepreneur in the family."

Nervousness roiled in Tess's belly as she thought of how much money her friend had already invested in her. Grabbing a pin from her belt, she tightened the neckline of a model's brightly colored shirt. "What if my collection is a flop?"

"A *flop*?" Hallie said indignantly. "At the Campania? Impossible! And we're raising money for charity. How can it go wrong? Serena is going to be a huge hit!"

Serena. Tess shivered. She'd named her company after her mother, and this show would raise money to fight the disease that had killed her. Another layer of pressure if she failed.

The last month had been a whirlwind. Since she'd returned to New York, Tess had spent hours in her new baby-friendly office working on her designs. In the evenings, Hallie and Lola had joined her with their babies, drinking wine and listening to Tess talk tearfully about her marriage. Naturally, her friends had taken her side.

"That so-called prince is the biggest jerk in the world," Hallie had said.

"Second biggest," Lola had mumbled, but wouldn't explain. After all this time, she still refused to reveal the identity of her baby's father, forcing the other two to wonder. Hallie thought the man might be a famous celebrity. Tess guessed he might be a married jerk, like her own father who'd abandoned her. But Lola refused to say, making Tess wonder if baby Jett's father was even worse than they imagined…

But how would Tess know? She'd been wrong about so much, first and foremost Prince Stefano Zacco di Gioreale. Grief still twisted her heart. How could she face the world without him?

"I'm scared," she said to her friends, whispering so the models and hairstylists and makeup artists wouldn't hear.

Hallie squeezed her shoulder, then turned to speak quietly to an assistant, who hurried out of the room.

"Stop whining," Lola said. "Your clothes are

good. You know they are. So just shut up and do it."

Slowly Tess walked past every model yet again, looking carefully at each outfit. Her clothes weren't expensive or intimidating. Instead, she'd created warm, colorful, comfortable outfits designed to make women happy, both with how they looked and how they felt.

Twelve outfits, each of them brightly colored, a mixture of old and new. She stopped at the very last model, who was wearing an ivory-colored wedding dress, embroidered with a small blue bird on the edge of the skirt. The bride held a bouquet of bright blue tulips.

Staring at the bouquet, Tess stopped, remembering her own wedding bouquet of pink roses. How happy she'd been, how sure that the two of them would live a fairy tale…

What was she saying? She'd wanted to kill Stefano with her shoe. She should have known a marriage begun in blackmail could only end badly.

And yet… A lump rose in her throat, and she had to blink back tears.

"Don't worry, Your Highness," said the girl in the wedding dress. "I won't let you down."

It was Kebe, the young model Tess had defended in Paris. When the girl had heard Tess was showing her debut collection in New York, she'd volunteered to walk the runway for free. She'd also promoted the event to her half-a-million followers on social media, causing the event to promptly sell out.

Tears rose to Tess's eyes at the girl's kindness even as she chided gently, "I told you, call me Tess. I'm not a princess anymore."

"You are to me," the girl said firmly.

"Tess?"

Turning around, Tess saw her uncle standing uncertainly in the doorway, holding baby Esme.

"Uncle Ray." Coming forward, she hugged him, then took her baby in her arms.

"Your friend—Mrs. Moretti—thought you might want to see Esme before the show," her uncle said awkwardly. He shook his head in amazement. "Look at you, Tessie. You're a designer. Just like you said you'd be."

Tess cuddled her baby in her arms. "I feel lucky."

"It's more than luck." Her uncle hung his head. "I should have believed in you more. Encouraged you."

She looked up at him in surprise. "You took me in, Uncle Ray. You gave me a home."

"I gave Serena a hard time, too. Because I never thought crazy dreams could actually come true." His eyes looked suspiciously wet. "But now, seeing you…it makes me wonder if maybe I should follow a crazy dream of my own." His voice became a whisper as he patted her shoulder. "Your mama would be so proud."

For a moment, Tess was too overwhelmed to speak.

Taking the baby back in his arms, Uncle Ray said gruffly, "We'll be cheering for you out there. Every step of the way." Smiling, he said to Esme, "Wait till you see all the amazing things your mama has done."

As Tess watched them leave, those words echoed in her ears. *Wait till you see all the amazing things your mama has done.*

At that, her shoulders straightened. Her fear melted away.

She wished—how she wished—that Stefano could have loved her. She still loved him in spite of her best efforts. No matter how many times she told herself that she'd loved an illusion. She loved the man he could have been, and suspected she always would.

But she'd be grateful for what remained. Her family. Her friends. Her daughter. She'd do everything she could to make them proud today. And even if she failed, she'd never stop trying.

"All right," she said firmly to the models. "Let's go!"

Tess hovered in the back of the large, elegant tearoom as the first model sashayed past the potted palm trees and gilded mirrors. The tea tables had been cleared out, replaced with a long catwalk surrounded by chairs.

The models entered one at a time, some of them dancing, all of them smiling. Music played, light-hearted and free. It was fun, playful, casual.

Tess blinked back tears as she watched the models wearing her designs. To her surprise and delight, with each new outfit, the audience's applause grew louder. Finally Kebe came out on the catwalk, gliding serenely in the wedding gown. The music built, and holding the blue tulips triumphantly over her head, she turned back to where Tess shyly hesitated.

"Come on, Princess!" she called. "Come up here!"

With a deep breath, Tess went out to face her public.

There was thunderous applause. She gave an awkward wave, then stopped as the tears in her eyes spilled over, as full as her grateful heart.

Perhaps she couldn't have what she'd wanted most. But at least there was this—this one moment—

She saw a flash of red as someone handed her a huge bouquet of red roses. Hallie must have arranged flowers. She looked past the long-stemmed red roses to smile at the person hidden behind them.

Then her breath left her.

It was Stefano.

Suddenly everything else fell away. The applause, the lights, the music, the audience. There was only now. This. *Him.*

"Stefano?" she whispered uncertainly, trembling.

Coming closer, he looked at her, and she saw that his dark eyes were luminous with tears. He said in a low voice, "You're a star. As you always deserved to be."

"What are you doing here?"

Dropping the roses, he took her hands in his own. His touch burned through her, and so did his dark eyes. "I'm here for you."

She looked up at him in shock.

Reaching out, he cupped her cheek. "You were right, Tess. I was afraid. I couldn't let myself love you because I couldn't bear the pain of losing you. Then I lost you anyway." Pulling her into his arms, he said softly, "Now I realize that there's only one thing in life that's worth any price."

The audience in the tearoom had fallen utterly silent. Even the models were staring at them. Tess held her breath.

"I'm in love with you, Tess," he whispered.

Now she knew she really was dreaming.

"You," she said, faltering and licking her lips. "You love me?"

"I've never felt this way about anyone. And I never will again. Just you. I love you." Stefano blinked fast. "You're all I care about."

Her heart was pounding in her throat. "What about Zacco?"

"I don't need it. Don't want it."

"What?" she croaked, nearly staggering back in shock.

"I just need you. You were right," he said huskily. "My legacy isn't a company. It's not wealth or power." He glanced at their baby, sitting with her aunt and uncle in the front row. He turned back to Tess, and this time there could be no doubt that there were tears in his eyes. "My legacy is you. You and Esme. And I'm yours."

"Stefano—"

"Give me the chance to show you," he whispered, and lowered his head to hers. His lips seared hers, hot and persuasive, gentle as silk. He kissed her tenderly, and when he finally pulled away, Tess blinked, lost in a dream.

"Can you ever love me again?" he said wistfully, running his hand down her cheek. "Can you?"

"I never stopped loving you," she choked out.

Joy lit up his eyes. Lifting her in his arms, Stefano whirled her around, making her colorful skirt fly out. She heard the audience's applause and sighs of delight. But, for Tess, it was just the two of them, laughing together with pure joy.

When Stefano finally set her down, his handsome face was bright. He kissed her again, and a moment later, Kebe and the other models came to congratulate them, and Hallie, too. Joyful music played as confetti rained down from the high ceiling amid the audience's thunderous applause.

"See?" Hallie whispered smugly in Tess's ear. "I told you the show would be a success."

Tess felt like her heart could burst. She waved at her family to join them onstage with Esme, then looked around for Lola, wanting her to join them, too. But she saw the blonde leaving with her baby, departing through the door on the other side of the room. She wondered what could be so important that would make Lola leave.

Then she forgot all about it as her husband pulled her in his arms, tilting her back with a fierce kiss.

"Is this really real?" Tess said in a daze, looking up at his handsome face as colorful confetti fell around them like flower petals. "Or is it a dream?"

"It's both," he said.

She smiled through her tears. "What will I dream about now that all my dreams have come true?"

Stefano took their baby from her uncle. Turning to Tess, he wrapped them both in the security of his powerful arms. His dark eyes were luminous with love and hope. "We'll find new dreams together."

With an unsteady laugh, Tess reached up and ran her hand over his rough, unshaven cheek. "I think that's the sexiest thing you've ever said to me."

"I love you, wife," he said huskily, instantly proving her statement wrong. Then he kissed her with all the sweetness and power of a dream that would last forever.

"Look, Esme!" Tess beamed as she pointed out the window toward the parade on Central Park West. "Santa!"

"She's just seven months old. I think she might be a little young to care about Christmas," Stefano said, smiling at them tenderly. Tess grinned back.

"It's never too soon to start family traditions."

They'd just bought their new co-op, and most of their furniture still hadn't arrived, but Tess had desperately wanted them to move in before the New York Thanksgiving Day parade in late November.

"So we can start our first holiday season right," she'd said. "Just think of all the memories we'll make!"

Of course, Stefano had agreed. He couldn't wait to make memories with Tess. In their bedroom. Tonight.

Coming forward now, he wrapped his wife and baby in his arms as they looked out the huge window at the view of the parade and Central Park beyond. The festive season had just begun.

Later today, friends and family would arrive for the traditional American feast of turkey and mashed potatoes and pumpkin pie. As their dishes and pots hadn't arrived yet—they were lucky to even have a big table and chairs—the meal would be catered from one of the city's finest restaurants.

Except for the desserts and rolls, of course. Those would be provided by Tess's family.

No longer Foster Bros. Bakery, it was changing to the Foster Sisters, as her two young cousins were eager to take over. They'd been bored by college, and had instead taken a loan from Tess and Stefano—at exceedingly generous terms—to buy the bakery from their father and mother, who'd just left to sail the world. The older couple, who'd always secretly yearned for adventure, were finally seizing the day.

It was never too late to change your life. Or to change yourself. Hadn't Stefano learned that better than anyone?

After his obsessive attention the previous month, his company, Gioreale, was running better than ever and had just hit its highest stock valuation in its history. Mercurio had received amazing press after hiring the respected, beloved designer, Aiko Sakurai. Mercurio's stock price had gone up. Zacco's had gone down.

But the Zacco brand now mattered as little to him as the Palazzo Zacco in Ragusa. Neither had anything to do with him, in spite of the name.

The name wasn't important, Stefano had realized. Only the *people*.

Every time he remembered his years—decades—of unspeakable loneliness, of hollow wealth and cheap pleasures as he tried to pursue a useless goal, he shuddered a little, and thanked fate for sending his wife to save his soul.

Otherwise, who knew? He might be married now to Fenella Montfort. Ice went down at his spine at the thought.

The woman had quickly recovered from Stefano's rejection and immediately started dating her company's new designer, Caspar von Schreck. It had only been a few weeks, but already there'd been public clashes, fights and rumors of infidelity on both sides. Another shudder went through Stefano.

He was so happy to be out of that world. And so thankful to be in this one.

He looked down at his wife, so soft and loving. The gold signet ring glinted on her left hand. It had been resized to fit her slender ring finger. "I don't want a diamond," she'd told him. "I just want this.

Because it's part of you." Remembering, Stefano's arms tightened around Tess as their baby suddenly giggled, waving her stuffed giraffe.

"Mama," Esme blurted out happily, causing Tess to squeal with delight, as she always did. Esme beamed proudly. It was a new trick she'd just learned a few days ago. Her first word.

"Dada," Stefano said coaxingly now. "*Dada.*"

Perplexed, Esme stared at him, her fingers in her mouth. Then she pulled her hand away.

"Mama," she repeated proudly.

"Good job, sweet girl," Tess praised, covering her baby's fat cheeks with kisses. Still giggling, his wife looked back at him. "I see you haven't lost your competitive streak."

"Never have. Never will. And since you don't want me to invest in your company—"

"Hallie and I are doing very well, thank you."

"Then I need some other goal. Something spectacular. Something that will impress you."

"Impress me?" she said teasingly, "Most men would think it was enough to run a multibillion-dollar company."

"It's practically running itself, thankfully, so I can spend more time with you and Esme. But a man needs more than money," he informed her loftily. "He needs a challenge."

Tess considered. "You could decorate the apartment. Hire the household staff you keep claiming that we need. Start that venture capital fund you keep talking about."

Stefano tilted his head, considering. Then he smiled. "Maybe later. For tonight, I've got something else in mind." He leaned forward. "This is what I have planned for you after the baby's asleep and everyone's gone home tonight…"

He whispered some very provocative things in her ear.

"Why, Your Highness," Tess said, pulling back with a blush. "I can't believe you'd say such things."

Stefano gave her a wicked grin. "Not just once," he informed her. "Twice."

Her eyes became round as saucers. "Are you serious?"

"Maybe three times, if I'm really on my game," he whispered, and lowered his head to kiss her.

Then the doorbell rang, and he reluctantly let her go. They went to answer the door, to welcome their friends and family for their first dinner in their new home—even Cristiano Moretti, who'd somehow become a friend.

"After all," Moretti had told him last week, shaking his head, "with wives like these, we men have to stick together, or we'll be totally bowled over." Stefano had nodded solemnly in agreement.

For the first time in his life, Stefano knew who he was meant to be. Tess had been right. A man wasn't measured by wealth or power or the quality of his enemies. A man was defined by his love for family and friends. By the strength of his heart.

Tess was right about all kinds of things, Stefano thought, his lips tracing a smile. He looked down at her tenderly. He must be very competitive. Because, as they opened the door to the welcoming cheer of friends, Stefano suddenly knew his spectacular goal: For the rest of his life, he'd love his family more than any family had ever been loved before.

* * * * *

Did you enjoy
The Heir The Prince Secures
by Jennie Lucas?

*If so, find out what happened first
in Hallie's story*
The Secret The Italian Claims.
Already available.

And look out for Lola's story
The Baby The Billionaire Demands.
Available November 2018.

*All in the
Secret Heirs Of Billionaires miniseries!*